Praise for *The Killing Hills*

"Crisp dialogue, bits of humor, an evocative look at the region and a stalwart hero elevate *The Killing Hills* . . . Offutt captures the nuances of those who call this part of eastern Kentucky home." —*South Florida Sun Sentinel*

"[A] true page-turner." —Caroline Leavitt, *AARP*

"[*The Killing Hills* has] deftly plotted short chapters, fast-moving story line, minimal characterizations and strong regional atmosphere."

—Joyce Carol Oates, *New York Times Book Review*

"Loyalty and betrayal slide back and forth in this tightly plotted, immaculately paced novel . . . *The Killing Hills* probes the darkness in both land and families, along with the limits of forgiveness. It's not just a fine and unforgettable crime novel. It's a heartbreak and a bond."

—Beth Kanell, *New York Journal of Books*

"Offutt is something of a poet laureate of the Kentucky hills. He knows the landscape in and out, and some of the best descriptive writing in this novel captures the feel of that countryside, hollers, broken-down houses, and all . . . for mastery of place and plot, Chris Offutt's work is always worth reading." —Lee Polevoi, *Highbrow Magazine*

"Quite aside from being one of our finest storytellers, in his first crime novel Chris Offutt reminds us as always of how much we've pushed away from us—the natural world, kindness, community—and that the time will come when we reach again and it's no longer there for the asking."

—James Sallis

"Offutt takes the reader on a tour of a place they never knew existed and might not exist for much longer. *The Killing Hills* is the most evocative novel I have read in many years." —Crimefictionlover.com (UK)

"One of Offutt's strengths is his familiarity with the area's folkways, flora and people . . . A rural noir with attitude to spare, *The Killing Hills* moves as briskly as a well-constructed miniseries, right down to its unanswered questions that carry the hopeful possibility of a sequel."

—Lauren Bufferd, *BookPage*

"*The Killing Hills* is part thriller, part bittersweet tribute to author Chris Offutt's Appalachian roots. The curious mix of elegiac prose, violence and quirky humor delivers a vibrant yarn that keeps readers engaged right up until the last uplifting page."

—Lorraine W. Shanley, Bookreporter.com

"Chris Offutt's novel *The Killing Hills* is a work of brilliant Southern noir." —Largehearted Boy

"This is not your typical murder mystery . . . A pleasure to read . . . Offutt's gift for nature writing imbues his tale with a rich sense of majesty that provides a sharp counter-point to the tragedies that unfold."

—Suzanne Van Atten, *Atlanta Journal-Constitution*

"Few writers today can boast of a body of work as wide-ranging and virtuosic as Offutt's. His novels and short stories bend genres and upend expectations . . . In all of his work, Offutt combines literary artistry with narrative momentum. *The Killing Hills* is no exception: A taut, gripping thriller, it also draws us deep into the lives of its troubled characters with wit, compassion, and insight . . . The same knack for propulsion, characterization, and snappy dialogue that made Chris Offutt a natural for Hollywood are on ample display in *The Killing Hills*. The sentences and chapters are crisp and crackling, the mood and tone dark and ominous but not devoid of humor. Put simply, the man knows how to keep the pages turning . . . The result is a novel that, like fine Kentucky bourbon, goes down easy and leaves a long, lingering burn." —Ed Tarkington, *Chapter 16*

"A story full of feuds, rivalries, and crimes hiding in plain sight, *The Killing Hills* is as poignant and powerful as they come." —*CrimeReads*

"Chris Offutt's *The Killing Hills* is a tense, thoroughly engaging read exposing a Kentucky hill country peppered with deceptive decency, deflecting manners and deadly trip wires all just waiting to snag the Army CID boots of Offutt's formidable hero, Mick Hardin. A relentless story crafted with elegance, empathy and propulsive suspense." —Stephen Mack Jones, author of the *August Snow* series

"The fine dark art of the noir simile springs from the amoral beauty of the Icelandic sagas . . . through the savant, poetic solecisms of Raymond Chandler, and drains into the rich, black soil of Chris Offutt's high holler novels . . . riveting."

—*Literary Hub*

"The lean prose elicits more than a hard-boiled style, and while the brisk yet gnarled atmosphere is reminiscent of *Winter's Bone*, the dime-store crime novels of Jim Thompson, or even William Faulkner's *Sanctuary*, Offutt brilliantly evokes the body and soul of his wounded hero. It adds up to a mesmerizing and nightmarish view of what lurks just over the hills. This is sure to be Offutt's breakout."

—*Publishers Weekly* (starred review)

"Acclaimed Kentucky writer Offutt [delivers] another fine example of what might be called holler noir . . . In place of plot convolutions, Offutt offers those of Appalachian folkways. The result is a fast-paced, satisfying read. Rural crime fiction that kicks like a mule."　　　—*Kirkus Reviews*

"Offutt superbly blends classic country noir and character study, [with] both great sadness and understated humor."

—*Booklist* (starred review)

THE
KILLING
HILLS

Also by Chris Offutt

THE KILLING HILLS

CHRIS OFFUTT

Grove Press
New York

The quotation on the epigraph page is from the poem "In Kentucky" by James Hilary Mulligan.

Published simultaneously in Canada
Printed in Canada

This book was set in 12-pt. Bembo by
Alpha Design & Compoistion of Pittsfield, NH

First Grove Atlantic hardcover edition: June 2021
First Grove Atlantic paperback edition: June 2022

Library of Congress Cataloging-in-Publication data is available for this title.

ISBN 978-0-8021-5987-8
eISBN 978-0-8021-5842-0

Grove Press
an imprint of Grove Atlantic
154 West 14th Street
New York, NY 10011

Distributed by Publishers Group West

groveatlantic.com

22 23 24 25   10 9 8 7 6 5 4 3 2 1

For Jane Offutt Burns

The moonlight falls the softest in Kentucky
The summer days come oft'est in Kentucky

    Friendship is the strongest
    Love's light grows the longest

Yet wrong is always wrongest in Kentucky

           —James Hilary Mulligan

THE
KILLING
HILLS

Chapter One

The old man walked the hill with a long stick, pushing aside mayapple and horseweed, seeking ginseng. It grew low to the earth obscured by the undergrowth. Last year he'd found several plants in this vicinity, an ideal habitat due to slopes that faced east, away from the hard sun of afternoon. The remnants of a rotting elm lay nearby, another good sign. He stopped to catch his breath. He was eighty-one years old, the oldest man in the community, the only old man he knew.

The ground was damp with dew, and tendrils of mist laced the upper branches. The rise and fall of morning birds filled the air. There were mostly hardwoods in here, trees he liked for their size and bounty of nuts. Cut and split, two trees were enough to keep a family warm all winter.

He moved upslope from the bottom of a narrow holler covered in ferns. Strapped to his belt was a pouch that contained ginseng plants with forked roots. One was large and sprouted three distinct prongs, each worth a pretty penny. He'd found several smaller plants but left them unbothered in the earth. They needed another year or two to grow unless a rival found them first. He carried a .38 snub-nose pistol. The accuracy fell away drastically after a few yards but it made one heck of a noise, and he kept it visible in his belt. The sight was usually enough to frighten any lowlife ginseng-poacher away.

He climbed to a narrow ridge, pushed aside a clump of horseweed, and saw a cluster of bright red berries. A quick jolt ran through him, the joyous sense of discovery he'd first experienced as a boy hunting ginseng with his brothers. He crouched and dug gently to protect the delicate root in case it was too small for harvest, which it was. Disappointed, he memorized the precise location for next year, noting the landmarks—a hundred-year-old oak and a rock cliff with a velvety moss, green and rusty red. Something caught his vision, a color or a shape that shouldn't have been there. He stopped moving and sniffed the air. It wasn't motion, which ruled out a snake. It might have been light glinting off an old shell casing or a beer can. Either one was no good—it meant someone else had been up this isolated holler.

Curious and unafraid, he moved through the woods, hunched over slightly, sweeping his vision back and forth as if looking for game sign. The land appeared undisturbed. He stood upright to stretch his back and saw a woman lying in an ungainly fashion, her body against a tree, head lolling downhill, face tilted away from him. She wore a tasteful dress. Her legs were exposed and one shoe was missing from her foot. The lack of underpants made him doubt an accidental fall. He moved closer and recognized her features well enough to know her family name.

He returned to the ginseng plant and knelt in the loam. He pierced the dirt with his old army knife and rocked the blade until he could lift the young plant free. Ginseng didn't transplant well but it was better than leaving it here to get trampled by all the people who'd arrive to remove the body. It was a pretty place to die.

Chapter Two

Mick Hardin awoke in sections, aware of each body part separate from the rest as if he'd been dismantled. He lay on his arm, dull and tingling from hours of pressure against the earth. He shifted his legs to make sure they worked, then allowed his mind to drift away. A few birds had begun their chorus in the glow of dawn. At least it hadn't been a bad dream that woke him. Just birds with nothing to do yet.

Later he awakened again, aware of a terrible thirst. The sun had risen high enough to clear the tree line and hurt his eyes. The effort to roll over required a strength that eluded him. He was outside, had slept in the woods, with any luck not too far from his grandfather's cabin. He pushed himself to a sitting position and groaned at the fierce pain in his skull. His face felt tight as if stretched over a rack. Beside him, three rocks formed a small firepit beside two empty bottles of whiskey. Better the woods than town, he told himself. Better the hills than the desert. Better clay dirt than sand.

He walked slowly to a cistern at the corner of the old split-log cabin and brushed aside a skim of dead insects from the surface of the water. Cupping his hands, he drank from it, the cold liquid numbing his mouth. He'd read about a scientist who talked to water then froze it and examined the crystals, which changed depending on what was said. Kind words uttered in a gentle tone made for prettier crystals. The idea sounded far-fetched but maybe it was true. Humans were about sixty percent water and Mick figured it couldn't hurt to try. Nothing could hurt much worse than his head anyhow. He plunged his head into the water and talked.

When he needed to breathe, he lifted his head to gulp the air, then shoved his head back in the barrel and spoke. He'd spent the evening telling himself terrible stories about his past, his present, and his future—a circular system that confirmed his wretched sense of self, requiring alcohol for escape, which fueled further rumination. Now he struggled to find generous things to say about himself. As he spoke, bubbles rose to the surface and he tasted dirt.

The third time Mick came up for air, he saw a vehicle at the edge of his vision and assumed it was something he'd imagined. He wiped water from his eyes. The big car was still there, and worse, there appeared to be a human coming toward him. Worst of all, it was his sister wearing her official sheriff's uniform. To top it off, she was laughing.

"What do you want?" he said.

"Oh," Linda said, "checking on your hygiene in general. Looks like you're bathing regular. Taking a bug bath, that's what Papaw called it. How you doing?"

"Feel like I been shot at and missed, shit at and hit."

"At least your head is clean."

Mick nodded, the movement sending stabs of pain along his body. His head felt like the top of a drum tightened bolt-by-bolt until any pressure might rip his flesh. He'd overdone it, all right.

"Coffee," he said. "Want some?"

He went in the house, water streaming along his torso and light blue chambray workshirt. He filled a blackened four-cup espresso pot with grounds and set it on a camp stove—a propane tank with stabilizing fins—and ignited the flame. Linda inspected a tin pitcher of water for bugs.

"Where's this from?" she said.

"Papaw's well."

"How long you aiming to live out here?"

"I need to change clothes."

Linda nodded once, a single curt movement of her head she used with most men. Everyone had their little ways, their routines. Mick's were odd, a product of living with their grandfather in this cabin as a child followed by fourteen years in the army. He'd been a paratrooper then joined the Criminal Investigation Division, specializing in homicide.

Linda moved languidly about the main room as if the space itself rendered time obsolete and slowed her motion. A homemade shelf bolted to a wall held the treasures of Mick's childhood—a trilobite, the striped feather of a barred owl, a mummified bullfrog he'd found in a shallow cave. A rock with three horizontal sections that resembled half a hamburger. Her grandfather had tucked blankets around her and pretended to take a bite—a moonlight ration, he called it. Linda grinned at the memory.

She went outside and followed a path to a wooden footbridge that crossed the creek to the next hillside. As children, she and Mick had built elaborate structures from sticks and leaves beside the creek, imagining it as a river town with a mill, rich families, wide streets, a hotel, and a movie house. Then they sat on the bridge and destroyed everything from above with rocks, delighting at a direct hit. The game was among her favorite memories but as she sat there now she realized that it marked a distinct difference between Mick and her. She'd liked creating the town while her brother had enjoyed its destruction.

He joined her with coffee and they sat with their legs dangling off the edge of the bridge. As usual, he waited for her to speak, aware that it wouldn't be long.

"That creek looked further away when we were kids," she said.

"We probably added another two feet of creek bed with the rocks we threw."

"I was just thinking about that."

"I know."

"So you can read my mind?" she said.

"Nothing else to do but sit out here and remember."

"You like the past that much?"

"Not lately," he said.

"What is this, some PTSD thing?"

"Right now it's a bad hangover."

"You think you've got PTSD?" she said.

"Probably. Dad did. Papaw, too." He blew on his coffee and took a sip. "Don't worry, I don't exhibit any sign of PTSD."

"Like what?"

"Like denial for starts."

She glanced at him, a sidelong shot of eyeball, trying to be circumspect but knowing he didn't miss a thing, not one damn thing, even hungover. His preternatural alertness made life hard for everyone, especially himself. She decided not to bring up his pregnant wife.

"You thinking about Peggy?" he said.

"How the hell do you know that?"

"It's logical is all. But she ain't why you're here, is it?"

"No, it's not. Since you're so good at knowing things, you tell me why I'm visiting you."

"That's easy, Sis. You came up here in uniform, driving the county vehicle, then waited around. You want something."

"Damn it."

Mick nodded, amused. He loved his sister, particularly her foul language. She'd been the first girl in the county to play Little League baseball, the first woman deputy, now she was the sheriff.

"I've got a dead body," she said.

"Bury it."

"They want me out."

"Who wants you out of what?"

"All the big shots in town," she said. "The mayor wants the Rocksalt police to take over so he can get credit at election time. The County Judge said he didn't like anybody in our family going back fifty years. He wants the State Police to investigate. It's jurisdictional bullshit. Pisses me off. The real reason is they don't like a woman being sheriff."

"So what. They don't have authority over you."

"No, but they answer to Murvil Knox, a big coal operator. He's slippery as chopped watermelon. Funds both sides in every election so he's owed no matter who wins. I had the awfullest meeting with them first thing this morning. About like three roosters in fancy clothes. I hate how men act around each other."

"To hell with them."

They stared at the creek. A breeze rustled the poplar, its leaves the size of hands turning their palms to the wind.

"This kind of murder," she said. "It never happened here before."

"What do you mean, Sis?"

"There never was a body in Eldridge County that most folks didn't already know who did it. Usually a neighbor, a family, or drugs. Maybe two drunks who argued over a dog. This is different. Everybody liked her. She lived clean, didn't have enemies, and didn't get mixed up with bad people."

"Odds are a man did it."

"I agree. You're a homicide investigator. You know the hills better than I do. People will talk to you."

"You asking for help?"

"Hell, no," she said.

He nodded, grinning.

"What have you got?" he said.

"A forty-three-year-old widow up on Choctaw Ridge. Off the fire road past Clack Mountain. Veronica Johnson, went by Nonnie. She was a Turner before she got married. Her husband died. Nonnie and her boy moved in with her sister-in-law. They both married Johnsons who died young."

"Go talk to them. Find out what the son knows."

"Done did. He's a wreck. Somebody took his mom up in the woods and threw her over the hill like trash."

"When did it happen?"

"Three days ago," she said.

"It rained yesterday and half the night. There's nothing to see at the scene. Rain washed all the tracks away. That's why I was outside."

"You like drinking whiskey in the rain and sleeping in it?"

"Yes."

"Why?"

"Because I couldn't do it in Iraq, Afghanistan, or Syria. No whiskey. No rain."

Linda walked to her car and returned carrying a manila envelope stamped with the official insignia of the county. Mick nodded, a habit she recognized from their grandfather. With the two of them in the same room—Papaw and Mick—they nodded more than those little bobble-headed dogs that people put in the back window of their cars. She hated being stuck at a red light behind one.

Linda handed him the envelope.

"Crime scene photos," she said.

"Who found the body?"

"Mr. Tucker. You know him."

"Grade school janitor? I figured he was dead."

"He's getting up there. His wife is sick. Taking care of her is what keeps him going."

Mick studied the photographs one by one, staring at each for a long time. After going through them, he set aside those of the body and gathered the photos from the dirt road. He spread them out on the mossy bridge and began moving them around as if seeking a sequence. Linda liked this side of him, the concentration he brought to bear, an intensity of focus. She'd seen it in pool players, bow hunters, and computer coders.

"What can you tell me?" she said.

When he spoke, his voice held a different tone, slower and at a remove, as if talking through glass.

"There's seven different sets of tracks. First car was his and the others drove over them. Who was up there?"

"Me. A deputy. Ambulance. County medical examiner. A Fish and Wildlife guy. A neighbor man who came to see what the fuss was."

"Who?"

"Fuckin' Barney."

"You talk to him?"

"No, I've been in court all week. A real mess. Couple of meth-heads had their granny living in a shed while they cooked in her house. I ain't had time to track down Fuckin' Barney yet. He's supposed to be living with his mother. I called her and she didn't answer."

"I'll go see her."

"I appreciate it," she said.

"I'm not doing it for you."

"Then who? Nonnie?"

"No, for the guy who killed her."

"I don't get it," she said.

"You know what Nonnie's family will do. Some old boy will take a shot at the killer, then get locked up."

"You're trying to keep a stranger out of prison?"

He looked at the creek bed below, watching a katydid nibble a blade of grass. His voice took on the distant tone again, like a church bell ringing down a long holler.

"I don't want nobody else to get killed," he said. "I had enough of it overseas. If I can stop it, I will."

As well as she knew her brother, Linda had no idea what he'd gone through in the desert. Like the other men in their family, he never discussed his experiences at war.

Mick stood and offered her a hand. She ignored it and they walked back to the cabin. Virginia creeper covered the western wall, the vines thick as a gun barrel.

"That can't be good for the wood," she said.

"It's worse around back."

"Do me a favor," she said. "Keep your cell phone on you for once. I called you four times."

He nodded. She watched him climb the rough-hewn steps to the porch, suppressing the urge to ask about his marriage. No sense aggravating him after he'd agreed to help.

Chapter Three

Mick ate four Advils, drank a quart of water, and went back outside, pushing the warped screen door to make sure it latched. Years of repairs gave it the appearance of an old quilt, patched by twine, spare wire, and a denim pants pocket. Mick's great-grandfather had built the four-room cabin by hand, solid construction with corners that still held true, the walls plumb, a floor as level as water. He'd picked this place due solely to the rough terrain. The hills were too steep and the hollers too narrow to log the woods. When Mick was nine his father died and Mick moved into the cabin with his grandfather, who was caring for his own elderly father. Linda stayed in town with their mother. The two old men taught Mick all they knew about the woods, wisdom that ran back to the Great Depression.

He found his cell phone in the truck. Four messages from his sister. No calls from his wife. Three missed calls from a number he recognized as an army base in Germany. His headache had subsided to a dull throb and he wanted to go to bed. Instead he headed toward Choctaw Ridge in his grandfather's old pickup, a 1963 stepside Chevrolet. If he felt good enough later, he'd go visit his wife.

Mick drove to the nearest gas station, a family business twelve miles away. Mick had known the Haneys all his life. A grandson ran it now, or maybe a great-grandson—each generation looked the same: stout through the torso with a set of shoulders like a fireplace mantle, powerful arms, and sturdy legs. Their heads were more rounded than elongated. All had ruddy expressions and the same thatch of unruly hair that started out red, faded early to gray and finally white. As a child Mick knew the patriarch, a man with snow-colored hair who went by Red. He parked in a concrete lot below the hand-painted sign that said HANEY'S BIBLE AND TIRE.

The youngest version approached the vehicle.

"I know that truck," he said. "Hardin, ain't it?"

"Yep, I'm Mick. Which one are you?"

"Joe."

"Big Joe or Little Joe?"

"Neither one. They're my cousins. They call me Little Big Joe. You wanting tires, gas, or a Bible? They'll everyone get you where you need to be."

"Top it off with regular. I got to go up a muddy hill. Got any junk laying around I can weigh the back end down with?"

"Got a Ford engine block weighs five hundred pounds."

"How much you take for it?"

"What'll you give?"

Little Big Joe let a sly grin wander his lips as he unscrewed the gas cap and inserted the nozzle. Mick nodded. He'd missed the swapping culture of the hills. Prolonged negotiations provided men an opportunity to display their knowledge without being show-offs. His grandfather could take a cheap pocketknife to a swap-meet and come home with livestock.

"I'll give you thirty dollars," Mick said.

Little Big Joe squinted as if in pain, letting the silence build until Mick offered more. Instead Mick cleared dead leaves and twigs from the tiny trough that held the windshield wipers, then polished the side mirror with his shirttail.

"Engine block is heavy enough," Little Big Joe said. "Won't shift around in the bed."

"Ort to work."

"Run you a hundred and twenty-five for it."

"Can't do it," Mick said.

"For fifty, I got axles and a busted woodstove. It's iron. But you'll have to get them on the truck."

"How about seventy-five and you help me load the engine block."

Little Big Joe finished filling the gas tank.

"Hundred," he said.

"Ninety."

"All right, but don't go around telling folks you skinned me out of it."

"I won't."

Little Big Joe's quick agreement on price meant he'd gotten the better of the deal, a fact confirmed by his request that Mick keep it to himself. He was protecting Mick from public indignity after taking advantage of him. It was the hill way. People looked out for each other even during conflict.

Thirty minutes later Mick left, the leaf shocks nearly flat from the weight. He'd sweated through his clothes while loading the engine and felt a little better. Acceleration was slow but he was confident the truck would make it up the muddy fire road. To get to Choctaw, he drove nearly to town before looping back along Lick Fork Creek. As he drove he thought about his sister. She was a Hardin, stubborn and tough, and Mick knew that the oblique request for help cost her some pride. He'd do what he could. Linda had begun her career in law enforcement as dispatcher for the town of Rocksalt's police force. Five years later the deputy sheriff was accused of sexually harrassing citizens. He resigned and Linda was offered the job because it would make the politicians look good. Four months ago the sheriff died of a massive stroke while fishing the Licking River and Linda was promoted.

Mick left the blacktop for a single-lane dirt road that rose and dipped with the land. Glade fern swayed near mudholes in the low parts while the higher sections held chickweed and groundcherry. The fire road was easy to miss and he slowed his pace, looking for the brief absence of trees, not the beginning of a road—one of his grandfather's lessons. Searching interfered with the ability to find. *Don't hunt for mushrooms, look for where they grow. At night don't look for an animal trail, just walk where the trees aren't. See shapes and colors, not the thing itself.*

This method of thinking served Mick well in CID. He investigated the same way his grandfather worked the woods—open to all of it, seeing what was there, and using the information to further his comprehension. The nuts of hardwood trees drew squirrels that were vulnerable to snakes coiled amid the undergrowth. Before gathering walnuts, his grandfather raked through the brush with a long stick to frighten away the snakes. Most bites were on the hand or foot. It was the same with people, Papaw had said. Mick didn't understand this until clearing rooms in Iraq and three comrades were shot in the hand by the enemy.

At the bottom of the fire road he inspected the deep ruts streaming with clay mud. If he was careful he could straddle the furrows and ascend the steep slope. The steering was imprecise from sliding tires but the weight of the Ford engine in the bed provided sufficient traction. At the top he stopped well back from the mess of tire tracks turned into mudholes from rain.

Mud sucked at his boots with each step as he walked to the edge of the drop-off and descended the hill to a narrow ridgeline. From his pocket he withdrew the crime scene photos and positioned himself to match their point of view. The body had lain at a thirty degree angle to the hill, against a towering elm, one of the few in the hills that had survived. The fallen leaves were dark-side up, having been kicked by EMTs and law enforcement.

Mick squatted and studied the earth, occasionally using a stick to brush aside undergrowth. He found two turkey feathers and a cache of hickory nuts forgotten by a squirrel. He returned to the place where the body was found and looked up the hillside. Visible was a honey locust beside a dogwood. He memorized their position, then climbed the slope to the two trees. If she was tossed over the hill from the top, she died close to where he stood. The leaves of a sugar maple were tinged yellow facing north, orange to the west. The land's beauty was undisturbed by death. Nature was used to it.

He drove toward town and stopped at a convenience store where he bought light bread, a tin of deviled ham, and a few cans of soup. A miniature hardware section offered plastic cases of nails that bent from the first blow of a hammer, an assortment of bolts and nuts that snapped under pressure from a wrench, and coils of wire so thin you could bite it in half. The prices were high and Mick wondered if the convenient factor applied to rich people who didn't know how to perform basic repairs. Thinking this way, he realized, meant he was feeling a little better. His headache was gone. He returned to the cabin for a nap.

Chapter Four

After dark Mick drove to town, followed Second Street west, and turned onto Bays Avenue. An older part of Rocksalt, the neighborhood was mostly residential with a few student rentals. The occasional porch light glowed. Visible through some windows was the blue flicker of televisions. Small bicycles lay in the front yards.

He parked beneath the swaying strands of a weeping willow, his wife's favorite tree and a significant factor for the purchase of their house. From inside he and Peggy could see the fronds moving with the slightest breeze. Now, tucked within the undulating tent of willow limbs, he watched the house, two windows lit from within, an occasional shadow indicating someone there—his wife.

In the early years of his service they'd explored Europe together, traveling by rail to small coastal towns, eating local fare and drinking wine in cafes. She was nineteen and he was twenty. Their life together had a sense of adventure but the constant transience of army life made it difficult for Peggy to find meaningful work. Due to small-town shyness, she was unable to develop swift friendships with other spouses, a bonding that was vital for military families. Mick requested a permanent post and was transferred to Garrison Baumholder in Germany. Wait time for housing was three weeks. Until then they stayed at the Lagerhof Inn, a military hotel. After a five-day argument, they decided to buy a house in Kentucky for her to live in year-round.

She was happier in Rocksalt and Mick was glad of it. He missed her on base but their time together stateside was cheerful and relaxed. His leaves in Kentucky had a romantic flair similar to when they first met. They organized elaborate dates in Lexington or set aside time to drive around with sandwiches, a sixpack, and folding chairs. They watched sunsets at Cave Run Lake.

Their new life worked well with texts and phone calls. They tried video chat but neither of them liked it. Due to the nine-hour time difference, one was always tired and talking in the dark. Last winter she took a job at a Lowe's home improvement store in Mount Sterling, a forty-minute drive one way. On their phone calls she had a fresh self-confidence and a willingness to laugh, both of which delighted Mick.

For eight months without a break he investigated a murder in Syria, a rape-murder at a garrison in Grafen-woehr, Germany, and two homicides at a Forward Operating Base in Afghanistan. Communication with Peggy began to dwindle—shorter emails, longer intervals between texts, and fewer calls. Mick blamed his twelve-hour days and a lack of consistent cellular reception. He solved the cases and returned to base in Germany. By then he'd had no contact with his wife for six weeks.

In the time-honored fashion of sisters everywhere, Linda texted Mick to call Peggy. He did and she didn't answer or respond to his texts. He called Linda who gave him the news—Peggy was pregnant, due to give birth very soon. Mick stood in the barren apartment he'd been temporarily assigned and performed a quick mental calculation. The math was right, coinciding with his last visit home in Kentucky.

"Mick," his sister had said. "Hello. You still there?"

"Yeah. How's it feel to be an almost aunt?"

"You need to talk to her."

"She's not taking my calls. No texts, nothing."

"I think she's scared. Doesn't want to bother you unless it's important."

Mick ended the phone call and requested emergency family leave from his commanding officer. The next day he booked a flight to Bluegrass Field in Lexington. A car service dropped him at his house and he stood in the driveway with his suitcase, grateful to be home. The house looked good but the gutters needed cleaning. Peggy stepped onto the porch wearing sweatpants and a large top that draped her swollen middle. She leaned against the door jamb as if exhausted. He'd never seen her hair so lustrous and thick. After a brief hug, awkward around her belly, Peggy retreated to the couch.

"You look good," he said. "It suits you."

"I can't get comfortable. I have to pee a lot."

"I wish I could do something to help you."

"Nobody can."

She adjusted her position as if in pain. He gentled his voice to assuage her misery.

"When are you due?" he said.

"Officially in two weeks. Could be three days or three weeks. The first one is sometimes late. I just want it out."

"Why didn't you tell me?"

She glanced at him briefly then stared at the rug that had belonged to her grandmother. It seemed like a river separating them. Her answer was too long in coming and his interrogation training kicked in. Something was wrong.

"Peggy," he said softly. "Why didn't you tell me?"

"I didn't want you to worry. I didn't want you to fly home upset."

Her words came fast and she still wouldn't look at him.

"Anything else?" he said.

"Yes, Mick. I made a mistake. I'm sorry."

"It's all right."

"No, it's not."

"People have kids all the time," he said. "We can do it."

"It might not be your baby."

"What?" he said. "What are you saying?"

"I don't know if you're the father, Mick."

Mick felt as if he'd been doused with kerosene and set on fire. His insides were abruptly hollowed out. The situation was simple but he couldn't quite comprehend that it was his situation, their situation. This kind of thing happened to other people. He wanted to get back on the plane to Germany. Instead he sat without moving, trying to relax.

"Tell me everything," he said.

She gestured to her belly.

"This is everything," she said.

"Talk to me," he said.

"It won't change nothing."

She looked about the room as if seeking something specific, a spot to settle her vision, a way out of things. He waited, deliberately opening his posture on the chair. He sank as far as he could, trying to bring his head lower than hers, an old trick to grant social dominance. It didn't work. She was sprawled on the couch which was already closer to the floor than his chair. He sat back up. At the Lexington airport he'd showered and changed into clothes he knew she liked, Lee jeans, not Levi's, a light blue shirt with short sleeves. Now he felt foolish for taking her preferences into consideration. If his marriage was this bad, he wondered how many other things he was deluding himself about.

He walked to the bathroom, instinctively scanning the surfaces for evidence of a man—a recently used razor, deodorant, a toothbrush. There was nothing, but she could have tidied up. He splashed cold water on his face and went back to the living room. Peggy had shifted on the couch, seeking comfort with an extra pillow, her bare feet propped on a stool. Her ankles were swollen.

"I'll be back in twenty minutes," he said.

He drove her car to a drugstore and bought a paternity kit. He scraped the inside of his mouth with a swab, then carefully inserted it into the plastic tube and returned to his house. Peggy had changed position again and was playing a game on her phone. He set the kit on the coffee table.

"Here," he said. "My DNA's in there already. Tell your doctor to draw blood, then you send it off."

"What?"

"Find out if the baby's mine. FedEx will pick the package up. Takes about a week."

He turned to leave.

"Where are you going?" she said.

"Papaw's cabin."

He left, wanting to slam the door but easing it shut to prevent startling her. He walked to a liquor store housed in an old railroad freight station. He'd always preferred Best Chance, operated by family members of a former bootlegger, an enormous man named Beanpole. He bought a case of bourbon and called a cab. The driver attempted conversation until seeing Mick's face in the rearview mirror, then gave up. At the far edge of the county he deposited Mick on a dirt road that was little more than a pair of ruts with weeds. Mick carried his load two miles and rested. He wished he had his rucksack. He wished he'd never come home. He climbed the hill to the cabin and drank a bottle of whiskey. For the next nine days he drank until his sister showed up asking for help.

Now he sat in the old truck behind the willow tree, wondering how to proceed. If he went to the door, should he knock? Should he call first? Did she want to see him? She was alone in a mess and needed a friend. His loyalty made him a good soldier, a good brother, and a good husband, but there was no clear path for moving forward. It was dangerous territory. Numerous times he'd entered unfamiliar buildings knowing that men inside wanted to kill him. He'd worn body armor and carried three weapons, spare ammo, a coms unit, and Israeli Battle Bandages. Now he was skulking around outside his own home, unprotected and afraid.

A car drove slowly past, turned at the corner in a broad fashion as if driven by an elderly person or a teen with a new license. A man walked a tiny dog on a leash. Mick recalled when they bought the house. They'd been happiest when painting the walls together, him on the roller and Peggy with a trim brush. They'd replumbed a bathroom which was simpler than he'd thought—not exactly easy, but the physics were straightforward—clean water in, dirty water out, gravity did most of the work.

He loved her. He would always love her. He'd never met another woman he liked as much, or seen one he thought was better looking. During sex, Peggy's face seemed euphoric, her mouth tiny, eyes wide as if drugged. That's what bothered him. Not the sex or the child growing in her womb, but the sheer injustice of another man seeing her face that way.

He decided to march across the lawn, knock twice, enter, and hug her. The moment he placed his hand on the lever of the truck door, he was riven by a fear deeper than any he'd experienced in combat. He turned the key, put the truck in gear, and drove to the cabin. For hours he lay on the narrow cot wishing he had a bottle of bourbon. He'd heard that time heals all wounds, which he knew to be a lie. Time didn't heal anything, it made you forget. Whiskey accelerated the process. Sleep eluded him until he imagined lying in his own bed in his own home beside Peggy.

Chapter Five

Shifty Kissick made her bed every morning, careful not to let the pillows rest on each other lest such a sight be too suggestive of sexual conduct. Though her husband had been dead nearly ten years she still maintained the habit. She'd had five kids, including one daughter who'd moved to Michigan when her husband got a job at a Ford plant. The family visited Shifty once a year but she couldn't make sense of her grandchildren's refusal to leave the house. They preferred to sit on the couch and watch each other play games on tiny flat screens.

During their last visit Shifty had placed a few tufts of grass in three jars and perforated the lids. With cookies as a bribe, she gathered her grandchildren outdoors at dusk, caught a lightning bug, put it in a jar, and gave it to the youngest girl. The two older boys began chasing the erratic bugs around the yard and Shifty remembered watching her sons do the same. When the hind end of the lightning bug glowed, her boys pinched it off and smeared the biolumi-nescence on their faces. They jumped at her in the dark and she pretended to be scared. It was a fond memory and she hoped her grandkids would try the same trick with her. To encourage them, Shifty squeezed the green glowing substance onto her fingers and dabbed her nose with a dainty gesture. The kids immediately released their lightning bugs and fled into the house. One boy was crying. "It's a living thing," he said. "You killed a living thing."

He didn't trust his grandmother for a day then forgot about it, but Shifty never trusted him again. She was irritated with her daughter for raising such children. She didn't even know what kind they were—city kids, she reckoned. Next they'd be stealing hubcaps and carrying switchblades.

For the most part Shifty enjoyed having the house to herself. She'd lived with her father until she was twenty-two and got married, then moved in with her husband. Shifty had never lived alone before and liked it. She could lie in bed and eat a roast beef sandwich if she wanted to. Neighbor women urged her to get a pet. She staunchly refused. Shifty had spent her life taking care of others—her father, her husband, the daughter who betrayed her by fleeing, and her four sons. She wasn't about to fool with a cat or a dog. She had, however, adopted a stray chicken and taught it to walk backward.

Her peace and solitude shattered when her youngest sons arrived, first one then the second. The older two boys were lost to her—one to the graveyard and the other stationed at Camp Pendleton in San Diego. For a while she worried about him in California with all those serial killers and vegetarians but she figured a Marine could take care of himself.

After tidying the house she opened the windows to air the rooms. She went outside and talked to Sparky but the chicken was in a bad mood and refused to cooperate. Shifty didn't mind, birds were moody in general. She would be, too, if her life was spent pecking at the dirt. A television program about ostriches had recently made her sad, trying to imagine the forlorn life of a flightless bird. With a great deal of chaotic effort, even Sparky could hurl herself onto a tree branch for safety. People ate ostriches—the TV said they were best cooked rare. All Shifty could think about was slaughter. She'd wrung the necks of many chickens but that would be impossible with an ostrich. Then you'd have to pluck the thing.

A plume of dust rose on the road and she heard the engine, an old truck in her opinion. A stepside pickup came into view, veering to avoid the low boughs of a crabapple tree. She knew the truck but couldn't recall whose it was. The driver stopped and got out. Unlike most men he wasn't wearing a cap and his hair was very short, uneven as if he'd trimmed it himself. He wore a short sleeve shirt that could stand a wash. He looked rough as a cob, badly needing a shave.

"Hidy, Mrs. Kissick," the man said. "I'm Jimmy Hardin's boy, Mick."

"That your daddy's truck?"

"Sure was. And his daddy's before that. You might've knowed my papaw."

"Heard of him. Can't say we met. I did know your daddy a long time back. You favor him some."

She looked Mick over, appreciating that he held his ground, waiting politely for an invitation onto her land.

"Catch that feller yet?" she said.

"Uh, who's that, ma'am?"

"Guy who stole your razor!"

He rubbed his stubbled jaw. She chuckled, then laughed.

"Ain't heard that one in a while," he said.

"Come on up to the porch. You want some coffee?"

Mick nodded and crossed the yard, alert to a dog but all he saw was a chicken walking backward.

"Your yard bird always do that?" he said.

"No, she don't. Might be showing off for company."

Shifty gestured to a nylon-slatted lawn chair with a TV remote control duct-taped to the arm. She went in the house, the screen door banging once, then settling shut, a sound she'd always liked.

The old chair creaked as Mick sat and stretched his legs, boot heels on the floor. The porch had a view of the dirt road, a line of weeds marking the creek, and the steep hill beyond the water. A breeze carried the scent of mountain mint from the side. The chicken had walked around the house and Mick wondered if it was back there practicing backflips.

Shifty set two cups of coffee on a small table between the chairs.

"Bet you're wondering about that TV clicker," she said.

"Hard to lose this way."

"That's right," she said. "When my boys are home they make a mess of everything. I got tired of digging for it in the couch."

"Your son is more or less why I'm here."

"Which one?"

"Uh, well," Mick hesitated. "Your second boy, I reckon."

"Oh," she said. "Fuckin' Barney. He ain't here right now."

"You call him that, too?"

"We're a nickname family. You know Shifty's not my real name, either. It's Camille Littleton, then I got married and my husband started in calling me Shifty because the only clothes I had were shifts my mother made. Now we got Cricket, Jimbo, Junebug, Sheetrock, Doodle, and Rickets."

"Rickets. Ain't that a disease?"

"Yeah, but he never had it. Just born bow-legged."

Mick sipped his coffee and grimaced. It must have been percolating all morning. He felt it hit his guts and begin bickering with the leftover whiskey. A wave of nausea passed over him followed by a sudden sheen of perspiration that covered his body.

"You smell that?" Shifty said.

"I believe it's me, ma'am. Drank a little too much whiskey a couple of nights ago."

"Thought so," she said. "It's not unpleasurable to me. My husband had the same smell on Sunday morning. My boys stink of marijuana most of the time. Do you smoke that stuff?"

"I tried it, yes. Didn't care for it. Made me nervous. Anybody else got relaxed and cheerful but not me."

"It gave me a headache."

"Maybe yours was just weak."

"That's what Fuckin' Barney said. But I never went for it again. I don't know when he'll be back but you can set here and drink coffee with me all day. Is he in trouble?"

"I ain't the law, ma'am."

"Your sister is."

Mick nodded, aware of her intent gaze. He attempted another sip. The coffee made his eyes water and he gave up. Shifty went in the house and returned with a small plate.

"Leftover sausage and biscuit from breakfast," she said. "You need to put a bottom to your belly. I like my coffee strong."

Mick ate, savoring the homemade biscuit and pork patty, then wiped his hands on his pants.

"What do you want my son for?" she said.

"A woman got killed on Choctaw a few nights ago and your son went up there. Maybe he saw a car. Them bigwigs in Rocksalt are on my sister over it."

"I'll tell him," she said. "Did you ever have you a nickname?"

"In boot camp, we all did. It ain't appropriate for me to say in front of a lady."

"I appreciate that," she said. "Been a while since I got treated with any respect."

"Thank you for the biscuit. It's the best I ever ate."

She smiled, erasing years of age. This was a woman who'd laughed a lot at one time and he hoped she still did. Mick stood.

"This is a pretty place," he said.

"Lived here most of my life. Went to Lexington once for a Wildcats game. Didn't like it."

"They lose?"

"No, they won. But I wasn't the only one who went that night. All them people in one place did me the way you said marijuana did you. I got real nervous."

He finished the last of the coffee, feeling it sizzle along his limbs. He stood, nodded to her, and went to his truck. She watched it vanish around the curve. Him coming up here was no good, she thought. No damn good at all. She went in the house and called her son to warn him.

Chapter Six

A few miles down the blacktop, Mick slowed for a man walking, then steered around him and stopped. Nobody hitchhiked in the hills. If a man was walking it meant he needed a ride because the journey was too long to cut through the woods. The man opened the door and climbed into the truck. He was a few years younger than Mick, wearing boots, jeans, and a workshirt buttoned at the cuff. The man kept his head turned, looking out the window as if shy.

"I'm Mick Hardin."

"I've knowed Hardins," the man said. "Went to school with one, Linda."

"That's my sister."

"Heard she's the sheriff now."

"Yep."

"Must come in handy if you get wild."

"It might," Mick said. "I ain't tested it yet."

"Saving up?"

"Reckon. No sense in wasting it. Who's your people?"

"I'm a Mullins. Bowling on the other side."

"Where you headed?"

"Up the road a piece. Third holler down, make a right."

Mick nodded. The road followed a creek strewn with trash clinging to the lower limbs of trees, deposited by high water from the last big storm. Most of the Mullinses he knew lived deep in the hills on high ridges. Such a location typically meant a strong desire to be away from town. Then again, they might be Melungeon people descended from the earliest inhabitants who already lived in the hills when Daniel Boone arrived. Nobody called them Melungeons any more, not even themselves, but the families were considered disreputable. Mick hadn't found that to be true. It was more a case of simple prejudice.

The man lifted his chin to point at the dirt lane that entered a holler and Mick slowed to make the turn. The road flattened through a stand of poplars that had been snapped by wind.

"Never did see an old poplar," Mick said.

"Worse tree in the woods. No good for burning or building. Ain't worth the trouble of logging them out. Storm knocks them down and then you got the work of clearing it."

"Other trees must like them. Or birds, one."

"Yeah, everything's got a reason if God put it here. Thing I think about is ticks. What are they good for?"

"Well," Mick said, "possums eat ticks. But I don't reckon they live on them."

"I like possums," Mullins said. "They're a funny animal. They got a pecker that splits in two at the end. I heard they fuck a lady possum in the nose and she sneezes out babies in her pouch."

Mick nodded. He'd loved that story as a kid and still did, despite knowing it wasn't true. He didn't want to get into it with Mullins. Disagreements like that had a way of getting out of hand in the hills, leading to a fistfight or gunplay.

He drove through a creek bed that was wet from the recent rains, rounded a curve up a hill and came to a house with a low front porch. One corner had a hickory post that supported the tin roof. The post on the opposite corner was missing. In its place was a mule with all four legs tightly tied to eyebolts screwed into the porch floor. A chain latched to the bridle kept the mule's head immobile. On its back was a wooden chair held in an upright position by a flank cinch. The chair's top rail supported the end of the porch.

Mick stopped the truck to prevent spooking the mule.

"Well," he said. "Never seen nothing like that."

"It's temporary."

"Do you use that chair for a saddle?"

"No, the mule came that way."

"What do you mean?" Mick said.

"My sister's got a boy courting her who likes to drink. Last night he run his car onto the porch and knocked the strut off. His daddy brought the mule over this morning.

The chair was already on him. He said he'd bring a new post later."

"What's its name?"

"Jo-Jo."

"Give you any trouble?"

"No, I reckon he thinks it's better than working. Only bad thing is that son of a bitch can piss like a horse. Mom hates it."

Mick chuckled and Mullins joined in as if seeing the mule for the first time. They sat in the truck cab laughing like teenagers. Mullins opened the door and climbed out.

"Thanks for the ride," he said.

"That mule don't look too comfortable."

"I'd say not."

"Maybe you can fix the porch."

"I'm a logger," Mullins said, "not a carpenter."

"Got any tools?"

"Hammer and nails, couple of screwdrivers and wrenches, same as any man."

"Measuring tape?"

"Naw, it broke."

"Can you find me a piece of rope?" Mick said. "Maybe ten feet long or more. And something to stand on."

Mullins nodded and walked to the house, giving the mule's back end a wide berth. Mick went to the porch. He stroked the mule's sweaty neck, sending a tremble throughout its body. The chain rattled and Jo-Jo's muscles strained against the hobbles. Mullins brought a coiled length of cotton rope outside. In his other hand he carried an old wooden milk crate from Spring Grove Dairy.

"Talk to him," Mick said.

"What do I say?"

"It don't matter. We got to keep him calm, so how you talk means more than what you say. Think of it like a horse that ain't full broke yet and you got to get a bridle on him. Talk quiet and steady."

Mick placed the crate beside the mule and stood on it.

"I had me a map once," Mullins said to the mule. "It was a good size piece of paper folded up. Red lines and blue lines and tiny print. Right here wasn't there, so I got rid of it. I figure the map didn't matter. The land knowed where the hills are at. North is Ohio, then some lakes and Canada. Out west somewhere is Lexington. You're lucky, Jo-Jo. You don't need a map. All you do is go straight, turn around, and come back. Then do it again."

Mick held one end of the rope to the porch ceiling and let the rest slowly uncoil. The mule quivered, its hooves stubbing the oak slats. Mick knew he was in a vulnerable position but believed the restraints would hold.

"Hey," Mick said softly. "Get that rope and hold it where it touches the floor. Don't pull it too tight. Cotton will stretch and throw us off."

"How tight's too tight?"

"Just hold it easy."

Mullins squatted to follow instructions. Mick climbed off the crate, opened his pocketknife, and cut the rope at the edge of the porch.

"Want me to keep on talking to him?" Mullins said.

"No. Go get your chainsaw."

Mullins stood, his face brightening under the familiarity of the task. He left and returned carrying a McCulloch chainsaw with a twenty-inch bar, oil glistening on the chain.

"Gassed up and sharp," he said. "But I ain't butchering that mule."

"Good to hear. Let's get in the truck."

They drove through the creek and along the dirt road to the line of broken poplar. Mick eyeballed several trees, settling on one that was straight and not too stout. He used the rope to measure the appropriate length, then told Mullins to trim the small branches and cut both ends flat. Mullins went to work, handling the chainsaw as if it weighed no more than a pencil. Mullins finished, pleased with himself. Mick rechecked the length with the rope and they loaded the denuded tree in the bed of his pickup and went back to the house. Jo-Jo hadn't moved.

"You favor a McCulloch over them other chainsaws?" Mick said.

"Never had no other. I started in using these because of a radio ad when I was a kid. It was on that Swap Shop show. Remember?"

"Maybe," Mick said. "How'd it go?"

He recalled it well but wanted to hear the jingle. Mullins jumped right into it:

"There is a reason why
Everybody wants to buy
At Monarch Supply
In Rocksalt . . .
McCulloch chainsaw!"

The advertisement had ended with the sound of a chainsaw starting, two mighty roars then the whine as it bit into a log. Mullins duplicated it as best he could and they laughed. A pair of starlings startled by human song angled away to a field by the house.

"Porch time," Mick said.

They carried the tree to the porch and positioned it behind the mule, out of kick range. Mick tipped it to the bottom of the two-by-six that supported the ceiling.

"Anybody else home?" Mick said.

"Mom and Dad."

"Go tell them not to come out here for a while."

Mullins did as he was told and returned. Mick was looking over the peculiarities of the mule harnessed to the porch, trying to decide the sequence of action. Each had risks of getting kicked. He unstrapped the hobble below the fetlocks on the front legs. The mule shifted, spreading its legs, and tried to rear its head but the chain held. Its back hooves shifted on the scarred slats, leaving fresh gouges.

"Easy now, Jo-Jo," he said. "Won't be long now."

"Hope he don't piss," Mullins said. "He'll about drown me."

Mick moved to the side of the porch and squatted. A steel clip held the harness chained to an eyebolt on the porch foundation. Mick leaned forward and released the chain. The mule whipped its head sideways and bit Mick in the forearm. He fell backward off the porch and rolled across the grass, smearing blood on his shirt. He stood and inspected the wound. It wasn't that bad, but not that good, either.

Mullins was laughing.

"That thing get vaccinated?" Mick said.

"I don't know. It ain't mine."

"I'll need to know. They carry rabies."

The specter of rabies halted Mullins's laugh like a door slammed shut. He nodded rapidly.

"Get some coal oil and duct tape," Mick said.

Mullins went to a shed and returned with a gallon jug lacking a label, half filled with orange liquid. Mick poured kerosene over the wound to clean it, then wrapped his T-shirt around his forearm, and secured it with duct tape. At least it didn't need stitches. Mick had been shot and stabbed, sustained a broken nose and cracked ribs, and carried shrapnel in his leg, but a mule bite was a first.

He stood at the edge of the porch beside the mule's back legs. The shackled pasterns were strapped to the floor with thick leather that was tied in a knot.

"I need a cornknife," he said.

Mullins hurried away and returned with the two-foot blade.

"Get back," Mick said. "I ain't sure what'll happen and I don't want to fight a mule."

He lifted the cornknife and chopped the hobble strap in two. The mule stood for a moment as if not quite comprehending its own freedom, then kicked each leg backward and leaped off the porch. The chair tipped sideways and shattered against a tree. Jo-Jo ran across the yard, jumped a rail fence, and disappeared into the woods. The roof sagged but the new poplar post kept it in place. Mick toenailed the post in place with eight-penny nails, the best Mullins could offer.

"I thank you," Mullins said. "Why'd you do all this? Feel sorry for Jo-Jo?"

"Look at it this way. If that mule had stayed hooked up to your porch too long, it wouldn't be no good for work. The father would blame his boy. Then the boy would come back around here mad at you. Likely to do something nobody wants. You'd have to do something back to him. Then my sister would get mixed up and somebody's setting in the jailhouse. So, no, it ain't necessarily for Jo-Jo, but the good of everybody."

"You think all them thoughts out when you seen the mule?"

"Pretty much, yeah."

"Damn, son, you're smart, ain't you?"

"Not smart enough to not get bit."

Mick drove to the house of the man who owned the mule, surprised to learn that he lived the next holler down. Jo-Jo was already in his own yard and Mick decided to stay in the truck. The neighbor man was short-waisted with powerful arms, and walked with a limp. He had vaccination papers from the vet, which relieved both of them.

Mick drove out of the holler. A crow in a sycamore tracked his progress as if on recon for the other birds. The road wove through the lush woods beside milkweed and Queen Anne's lace bent from heat. Aside from his throbbing arm, it was a pretty good morning in the hills.

Chapter Seven

Linda sat in her office waiting for the twenty-year-old fax machine to rattle its way through a document at two minutes per page. The phone system was push-button and the computers were so old and big they occupied a third of the desk space. Most of the county equipment was military surplus including an armored truck weighing twenty tons that had cracked the concrete parking lot upon delivery. So far its only use had been at a charity event in which groups of men competed to pull it with rope.

Until this week she'd enjoyed her private time in the office, its spartan decor of desk, filing cabinets, Kentucky flag, and a portrait of whichever nitwit had bought his way into the governor's job. She kept it tidy and organized. No personal items on display. The office had a door—a big deal in a small municipality—that she kept open most of the time. At night she locked it, always taking one final fond look at the brass plate with her name on it. Now she had a dead body and pretty much hated everything about the job.

Her first week as sheriff she'd appointed Johnny Boy
Tolliver as deputy. Due to a long and violent feud, the Toll-
ivers had gotten off to a rough start a hundred years ago, but
his branch was more or less accepted by the fifth generation.
Johnny Boy could talk to anyone at any time about any subject. This trait was a boon in a culture that was suspicious
of a female sheriff. Most surprising to her was the resistance
from older women who didn't trust Linda any more than
the men did. That didn't make sense but neither did waiting
on an antique fax machine to emit sheets of paper as glossy
as magazine pages.

Johnny Boy was lurking around the main part of the
sheriff's office, walking past her door now and again, like a
hunting dog letting her know he was raring to go. At least
he didn't whine like a hound, but he did talk too much
as a human. The fax machine stuttered and clanked, then
stopped altogether, a sheet of torn paper poking out like a
flag of surrender. Linda cursed and yelled for Johnny Boy,
who appeared in her doorway with sudden alacrity.

"What happened," he said. "Fax get hair balls? Maybe
I can take a look. Sometimes I can fix things. Today might
be the day. Good thing I'm in a fixing mood."

"I'm going over there."

"Want me to stay here?" His voice had a hopeful tone.
"Man the phones? Anything could happen, you know."

"No, you better come and hear it, too."

She called her brother and asked him to meet them
at the coroner's. Mick grunted and ended the call. Par for

the course, she thought, knowing he'd be there. Linda and Johnny Boy drove two miles to a funeral home that doubled as the county coroner's office. Johnny Boy was silent and she was grateful. He didn't like funeral homes. Nobody really did, but his trepidation veered into the fearful. He believed every superstition that came down the pike.

On the way they met heavy traffic which explained why the coroner had sent a fax. A proliferation of cars in Rocksalt could only mean a funeral unless it was Saturday morning and the kids were playing organized soccer. The parking lot held a few cars clustered near the entrance, spaces reserved for the family of the deceased. She parked and stayed in the car. The last thing anyone needed was a sheriff at a service. People would talk. Her predecessor had often waited in ambush to serve a summons, knowing that a funeral brought everyone in the family, even the fiercest outlaws hiding in the woods.

"Who died?" she said.

"One of them Fatkins boys," Johnny Boy said.

"Ain't they young for it?"

"They're getting down to the younger ones. Eight kids and five dead already. Heart attack and he ain't but forty-six years old. Left four kids and six grandbabies. He worked up in Lexington putting in culverts. I'd say three hours of driving and eight hours in the mud got to him. He done that for twenty-three years. His third heart attack, too."

"You got a head for numbers, Johnny Boy."

"Always was good at math," he said. "And I like to read obituaries. All kinds of information in them."

"Which one was it who died?" she said.

"Face."

"Who names their kid that?"

"Well, the Fatkins, that's who," Johnny Boy said. "You know the rest of the country lives longer than us. Or we die younger."

"What?"

"Life span," he said. "Everywhere else, folks live a little bit longer every year. Our lives are getting shorter on average. Ain't nowhere else in the country that's happening. Twenty years ago the life span here was longer."

"The hills are killing us."

People began emerging from the double doors, moving slowly, a few children running toward cars. A couple of teenage boys appeared from behind the building, probably back there sneaking cigarettes. Last to leave was the mother, supported on either side by younger women. Linda watched the Fatkins family drive away. Mick's truck rolled into the lot and parked beside her, the window rolled down.

"Perfect timing," she said to Mick.

"I was waiting out on the road."

"That little grassy place?" Johnny Boy said. "It's a good spot all right. You can see across that field. Ponies in there sometimes and sunflowers. I seen a flat cloud once that was a half mile long and skinny as a fence rail. Like a white stripe on the sky."

Mick rolled his window up and Linda told her deputy to hush. The three of them walked across the blacktop, fresh by the looks of it, yellow stripes still gleaming. The funeral home was broad with a high peak like a shingled pyramid. Up the hill behind it was a long building painted white. The flat roof had a sign that ran its entire length with the word MOTEL in seven-foot letters. Next door was a fast-food place that specialized in deep fried goods.

"That's new," Linda said to Mick. "Our first motel."

"Eat, sleep, and die," he said. "All in a convenient location."

"What happened to your arm?"

"Mule bite."

"Lucky it wasn't a snapping turtle," Johnny Boy said. "They won't let go till thunder hits. Sometimes you have to wait a week for a storm. Is that duct tape? Might not be sanitary. Want me to take a look at it? I took a course in field medicine up in Frankfort. Learned all manner of thing."

"Can you do anything about him?" Mick said.

"Not really," Linda said.

"Hey," Johnny Boy said. "I know y'all are brother and sister but you don't have to talk about me like I'm some-where else. I'm standing right here."

"We know that," Linda said.

Inside, she led them through the foyer and down a corri-dor past the empty viewing room. They passed a small office where a woman was entering calculations into an old-time adding machine. Her hair was swept up so tightly it served as a face-lift. Johnny Boy moved in a furtive manner then waved to her eagerly as if grateful for seeing a live person. They went to the back and knocked on a door with a sign:

MARQUIS SLEDGE III, FUNERAL DIRECTOR

Four plush chairs stood against the wall. The Sledges had buried everyone's people for fifty years, a family business founded when the grandfather returned from Vietnam with mortuary skills, a deepened belief in Christianity, and a desire to serve the community. As with all small towns, rumor and gossip was rampant about an undertaker. Due to Mr. Sledge's commitment to family and church, the usual unsavory stories faded to nothing. One persisted—an odd one in Linda's book—people said there was another Marquis Sledge, an African-American who ran a funeral home in Memphis.

The local Mr. Sledge died and his son took over, serving as County Coroner for thirty years. When Marquis Junior retired, his son ran unopposed for the position. His first change was to eliminate a form of advertising people didn't like—congratulatory notices to parents of newborns. They were unpleasant reminders that the baby would eventually die and the Sledges wanted their business.

The door opened and Marquis stepped out wearing a deliberately inexpensive suit with black shoes. His expression shifted from appropriately dolorous to slightly rueful.

"Sorry to send a fax," he said.

"The machine gave out before I could read it," Linda said. "Thought I'd just come over and get it straight. Hate to interrupt a funeral."

"I'm done for the day," Marquis said. "That Fatkins family has some bad luck."

"They'll be asking for a discount," Linda said.

"Already gave them one."

"You know Johnny Boy," she said. "This is my brother Mick."

Marquis nodded to both men, having learned from his father never to offer a hand for a shake. Nobody liked to touch a mortician. Mick startled him by sticking his hand out. Johnny Boy stared at the floor.

Marquis led them down the hall where he unlocked a heavy steel door and gave them nitrile gloves. In the center of the room stood a metal table beside a counter full of specialized tools. Johnny Boy stared at them, swallowed hard, and looked away. Marquis folded back the corner of a sheet to reveal a woman's head propped on a rubber block.

"Cause of death was asphyxiation," he said and pointed to discoloration on the neck. "Cyanosis is present."

"Turning blue," Linda translated for Johnny Boy.

"Right," Marquis said. "No ligature marks. Nothing to indicate strangulation by the hands."

"Defensive wounds?" Mick said.

"None."

"There's something else," Marquis said.

Johnny Boy's frown distorted his face into a look of horror. His breath was coming in quick short bursts. Marquis stared at the deputy and spoke in a firm voice.

"Don't you get sick in here, you hear?"

Johnny Boy's head twitched in a nod. Linda wondered if he was going to faint. His loose jeans prevented her from seeing if he'd locked his knees to stay upright. She pushed a work chair on casters toward him. He sat and placed a small trash can on his lap.

"She'd had sexual intercourse," Marquis said.

"Rape?" Linda said.

"Hard to say. Even consensual, it can result in some tearing of tissue, maybe bleeding. That's present. But it's not clear if the sex was forced."

Johnny Boy gagged into the trash can.

"Gosh darn it," Marquis said.

"Any semen?" Mick said.

"No trace whatsoever. No DNA. Abrasions on her body are all postmortem. Probably from falling down the hill."

"Could she have been killed then moved up there?" Mick said.

"There's always a chance," Marquis said. "But doubtful. The postmortem wounds occurred soon after death. My best guess is she died on that ridge, before, during, or after sex."

Johnny Boy retched and Linda pushed the chair into the hall. When she returned, Marquis had exposed the dead woman's hands. Mick was examing the nails, two broken, one cracked, the rest intact.

"No skin cells under her nails," Marquis said.

"Could be she knew the killer," Linda said.

"Anything else?" Marquis said. "I've got paperwork and cleanup."

"No," Linda said. "Thanks for squeezing this in."

Marquis nodded solemnly and Mick wondered if he practiced serious expressions in front of a mirror.

"One thing," Mick said. "If you could keep that sex angle to yourself, it might help us."

"I keep everything to myself," Marquis said.

Mick and Linda left. In the parking lot, they could see Johnny Boy leaning against the police vehicle holding his stomach, his face blanched. Linda asked her brother to meet them at the sheriff's office.

"No, thanks," Mick said. "You tend to Johnny Boy. What's wrong with him? He's seen bodies before."

"He's afraid of ghosts. Thinks a funeral home is full of them."

"People don't die in there."

"I told him that," she said. "What'd Fuckin' Barney have to say?"

"He wasn't home. His mom's all right."

"What happened to your arm? I mean for real."

"Like I said, a mule. Ain't worth going into. Them Mullinses."

"Which bunch?" she said.

"Off Little Perry Road, way up a holler."

"They're shirttail cousins of ours."

"Already knew that," he said.

"To hell you did."

"In the service I had access to all kinds of info. One day I looked up our family tree. A monkey shit on my face."

Linda laughed, a spontaneous eruption as if a water balloon exploded, dousing them both with merriment. Mick grinned at his sister. She didn't laugh enough. He recalled daylong efforts at drawing a giggle out of her when they were kids. She still laughed the same way, a sudden burst. It lightened her mood but afterward she hardened up more as if vulnerability cost something on an invisible tally sheet.

"How's Peggy?" she said.

"Stay out of it."

Mick got in his truck and drove away. Linda watched him, wondering if she'd gone too far.

Chapter Eight

Johnny Boy sat in the official vehicle, having mostly recovered from his nausea. Between dead bodies, ghosts, the undertaker, and Linda's hard-ass brother, he needed the icy comfort of a Dr Pepper. A mini-fridge at the office contained three bottles. Linda climbed into the car.

"Did you hear everything Marquis said?" she said.

"You mean the sex stuff?"

"Yeah. What do you make of it?"

"I can't talk about that."

"Because I'm a woman?"

He nodded and looked out the window. The weathered posts of a wire fence flashed past in gray blurs that reminded him of ghosts. He turned back to the windshield and focused on a large cloud above the hill.

"We are law enforcement professionals, Johnny Boy. You best remember that. If we have to talk about a man getting his peter bit off by a rattlesnake, we do."

Linda pressed the accelerator to the floor and the SUV shot forward as if flung from a slingshot. She smiled to

herself. Johnny Boy couldn't abide speed unless he was driving, some kind of control thing, she figured. He grabbed
a support handle above the door. A quarter-mile of fresh
blacktop stretched ahead and Johnny Boy's back pressed
hard against the seat, his face set in a grimace. They reached
the town limits and drove to the sheriff's office. A car she
didn't recognize was parked in the lot, a Lexus with Fayette
County plates.

"You know that rig?" she said.

"No, I don't."

"It's that damn Murvil Knox."

"The big coal operator?" he said. "He thinks so much
of his own hide, he'd gut himself to keep it."

"Yeah," she said. "He hates me."

"I hate his car. A Lexus is nothing but a Toyota whose
shit don't stink."

They were still laughing when they entered the office
and found Knox sitting at Linda's desk, pecking out a text
on a cell phone. He wore the standard outfit of a politician attempting to present himself as a man of the people
at a VFW fish fry. Beside him stood a young stranger in
stiff new khakis with zippered pockets on the legs, tactical
boots suitable for a city, and a dark sportscoat. Strapped to
a skinny belt was a holstered Glock and two spare clips.
Johnny Boy took a half step back, glad he wasn't the sheriff.

"My office, Mr. Knox," Linda said. "My desk."

Without shifting focus from the tiny screen of his
phone, Knox lifted a finger in the universal sign of "wait."

He pressed SEND, stood, and extended his hand to Linda, a wide smile spanning his face as if stapled to his head. He ignored Johnny Boy.

"Good to see you again, Sheriff," he said.

She nodded, shaking his hand. Long accustomed to the ways of men, she maintained a daily regimen of exercises to strengthen her grip. Sure enough, Knox immediately began pressuring her hand to demonstrate his manliness. Linda squeezed back, feeling the strain in the corded muscles of her forearm. He relaxed his grip like a dog rolling over to expose his belly and she knew he'd resent it forever.

"Mr. Knox," she said. "Do you have a crime to report?"

"Oh, no," he said, emitting a short fake laugh. "I wanted to personally introduce your new man. Special Agent Wilson from the FBI will be assisting your homicide investigation."

"I don't believe I asked for assistance."

"It's a favor to the county," he said.

"I'm comfortable with my deputy."

"Accepting Wilson will be doing me a favor."

"I'm not a politician, Mr. Knox. I don't engage in logrolling."

"I heard you were smart," he said. "Still, you have an election coming up and a few friends can't hurt."

"Friends like Wilson?"

"Friends like me," he said.

Linda waited, knowing Knox would fill the silence. On average, men tended to interrupt a woman after eight seconds. If a woman didn't talk, most men couldn't last four seconds, according to social scientists with government funding and a stopwatch.

"Being independent," Knox said, "is good. It's necessary in law enforcement. I understand that. You need to bear in mind we have the same goal. Making the county safe for law-abiding citizens."

"What are Mr. Wilson's qualifications?"

"Military service. Top of his class at the FBI academy. Six months' experience at the Pentagon. And he's from the area."

"I don't have an available desk or vehicle."

"That kind of budgetary concern is one of those things a friend like me can help you with in the future. He doesn't need a desk, right Wilson?"

"No, sir," Wilson said. "A table shoved in a corner is fine. I worked out of a broom closet in DC."

"He's flexible," Knox said.

"We don't have a broom closet," Linda said. "But I see your point. Was there a lot of murder at the Pentagon?"

"No, ma'am," Wilson said.

"This will be his first," Knox said. "Every man has to start somewhere. And every woman, too. If she's up to it."

He gave her a pointed stare and left the office with the air of a busy man, a mover and shaker, a man so high-collared he couldn't see the sun except at noon. Linda listened to the front door opening and closing. His self-important steps continued across the parking lot.

Wilson appeared to be age twenty, but had to be older if Knox was telling the truth. Men like him lied like a dog with no legs. She deployed the deep breathing techniques intended to calm her with little effect. She circled her desk, and stared at Wilson, hoping if she was silent long enough he'd leave.

"Where you from?" Johnny Boy said.

"Haldeman County," Wilson said.

"I played football against you all in high school. Leopards, right?"

"No, I went to Breck."

Johnny Boy glanced at Linda, his face abruptly closed over like a holler clogged by grapevines. She tipped her head toward the door and Johnny Boy quickly left.

"Just so you know," Wilson said. "I didn't ask for this assignment."

"What's Knox got to do with it?"

"A local contact, I was told."

"Are you reporting to him?"

His tense silence meant yes, as did the slow flush that tinted his neck and rose along his face. She was reminded of dyed chicks sold by the dime store at Easter. They all died by the end of the month, poisoned by the dye.

"You're my first FBI agent," she said. "What do you want?"

"Your incident report."

She opened a filing cabinet and removed a file. He took it as if handling a rare egg.

"When you're done," she said, "bring it back to me."

"Where should I read it?"

"Up to you, but don't leave the station or make copies. I'd avoid my deputy's desk. He seems to have taken a disliking to you. Why is that?"

"My high school didn't have a football team. Too small."

She nodded, thinking that men never got over their childish obsession with sports. The town of Rocksalt had gray-headed men who met at a liquor store to drink beer and trade on the glory of their high school exploits. Every time a customer entered they turned their heads in tandem, hoping it was someone who'd remember them.

Chapter Nine

The morning sun hauled itself up the hill and across the ridge, triggering the birds to begin their territorial calls. For the first time in a week, Mick had no headache, nausea, or fatigue in his limbs. He rolled over to sleep more, but once awake, he remained that way, his consciousness engaged. He thought of Peggy and tried to force her from his mind by stepping outside and cleaning mud from his boots with a knife. He thought of the sticks he'd used as a child to scrape dirt from his high top Converse shoes. In thirty years, all he'd gained was better footwear and a more efficient tool to clean them.

He got dressed, and drove off the ridge. At the blacktop he headed west. Nonnie Johnson had lived with her sister-in-law up a holler that followed a creek and became narrower the farther he drove. An oak bridge crossed the water, the timbers gray from weather. Beyond it the road ended at a well-kept grassy yard. He parked beside two cars and a late-model Ford F-150 four-by-four. A barking dog ran from the house, notifying the occupants of an intruder and warning Mick to stay in the truck. He rolled his window down and waited.

The screen door opened and a man came out carrying a .38 pistol with a long barrel, the gun pointed down at a slight angle. A quick snap of the wrist would bring it level with Mick.

"Real sorry to hear what happened," Mick said. "I'm Jimmy Hardin's boy, Mick."

The man lowered the pistol a little more and walked to the truck, his fierce gaze never leaving Mick's face.

"Never seen you up this holler before," the man said.

"I been away. Army."

"Iraq?"

Mick nodded.

"Is the desert hot as they say it is?"

"Yeah," Mick said. "About like being in hell with your back broke."

"You out now?"

"On leave. My sister asked me to come up here. She's the sheriff."

"What does she want?"

"Well," Mick said. "In a case like this, somebody has to talk to the family."

"We done did."

"Damn Staties got my sister running around. If you'uns don't talk to me, they'll get a warrant for you to come to the station in town."

The man spat a dollop of chew in the dirt. A bottle fly swooped down as if waiting for a snack. Disheartened by the tobacco, it departed. Mick opened the truck door.

"I'm not armed," Mick said. "You don't need that pistol."

"It ain't for you," the man said. "Whoever killed Nonnie might come back around."

"Shows good sense."

Now that he was out of the truck, gaining control of the pistol would take two seconds tops.

"Was Nonnie your aunt?" Mick said gently.

"How'd you know?"

"Just a guess. Do you think I could talk to your mom a minute?"

The man held the gun to his side casually as if carrying a duffel bag and gestured with his head toward the house. Mick climbed the steps. They were new, painted gray. The screen door was new, too. Someone was looking after the place.

The front room held an old couch with broad flat arms, the brocade worn to a nub, three chairs, and a TV set. A picture of a blue-eyed, blond-haired Jesus hung on the wall by itself. On another wall was a display of family—school pictures of kids and a few black-and-white photographs of serious people in their finest clothes. A narrow set of steps went upstairs. The man walked down the hall toward a back room where Mick could hear low voices.

A woman emerged from the kitchen. She was in her forties, heavy-set, wearing a loose dress and slippers, her long hair pulled back in a clasp.

"Are you hungry?" she said. "Them boys ate me out of eggs but there's a biscuit if you've a mind."

"No, thank you, Mrs. Johnson," Mick said.

"Just call me Lee Ann," she said. "You say you're a Hardin?"

Mick nodded.

"I know your people." She nodded in confirmation of the quality of Mick's family. "Set down a minute."

Each chair was worn in a specific fashion with dents on the headrests at varying heights. He sat on the couch, figuring it was for guests. Lee Ann brought him a cup of coffee.

"Thank you," he said. "I'm sorry about your sister."

"She's with Jesus now."

Mick blew on the steaming coffee, knowing he'd scald his tongue if he drank. The voices in the back rose again, strident as salesmen.

"I'm wondering if you could tell me anything," Mick said. "Maybe something you'd not want a stranger to know."

"Like what?"

"Like who might be mad at Nonnie. Trouble her boy had with somebody, or maybe your own boys."

"I don't think so, no."

"What about at work?" Mick said.

"She was a cashier at the Dollar General. They ain't much to get into there."

"Maybe a problem with the boss or somebody she worked with."

"No, everybody liked her. She talked to all and sundry."

"Was Nonnie mixed up with somebody? I mean, did she have a gentleman caller or anything like that?"

The woman tugged at her sleeve, tapped on her chair arm, and stared at the floor.

"No," she said in a firm voice. "Nobody."

The voices in the back rose again, overlapping as if in argument or to make a point. Mick sipped the coffee, breathing through his mouth to cool it. The woman shifted her vision from him to the picture of Jesus, and Mick figured she'd had years of practice at silence.

The door opened at the end of the hall, releasing the end of a conversation.

"Ain't got no choice," a man said.

"Nobody else but you for it," said another.

The door closed and three men in their late twenties came into the room, two of them identical twins. Mick stood and nodded.

"I'm Mick," he said.

"I'm Wade," the older one said. "These are my brothers, Noel and Joel."

"I done met one," Mick said, grinning. "Ain't for sure which."

"I couldn't tell them apart till they were five years old," Wade said.

"I could," Lee Ann said. "Joel's cowlick is about a half inch over from where Noel's is at."

"You always say that, Mommy," one of the twins said.

Mick nodded and drank from the coffee cup.

"If it's all right with you," he said, "can I talk to Nonnie's boy?"

"Frankie's pretty tore up," Wade said. "Won't hardly leave the bed."

"Don't blame him," Mick said. "Seems normal enough."

"Naw," one of the twins said, "he was already low. Been down for a couple of years."

"That why he was living here?" Mick said.

The brothers glanced at each other, frowning. Wade took a step forward, his voice hardening.

"Someone say something on Frankie?" he said.

"No," Mick said. "It's in my family. My uncle called it the 'can't-help-its.' Sometimes he didn't do nothing for months. Wouldn't leave the house. Wouldn't wash or eat."

"Losing his mom chopped Frankie down like a weed," Wade said.

"I'd still like to talk to him."

Mick looked at each man briefly, then settled on the woman. The final word would come from her.

"Might do him good," Mick said.

"Well," she said, "it sure can't hurt."

Wade stepped aside and Mick walked down the hall, hearing the brothers follow. He tapped on the door and went in. The room was small with an old-time standing wardrobe instead of a closet. On the bed lay a young man curled like a child, hiding his face. He wore longjohn drawers and a T-shirt. A quilt covered his feet.

"Frankie," Wade said. "Man here wants to see you. Mommy said it was all right."

Frankie didn't move or speak. Curtains covered one window except for a vertical slit that let in a slice of light. A cardinal called outside, cheerful as ever.

"Frankie," Mick said. "I'm trying to find out what happened with your mom."

"Go away," Frankie said.

"I want to help."

"Leave me alone."

Frankie yanked the quilt over his head. Mick left the room, thanked Lee Ann, nodded to each man, and left. Outside, Wade stood beside the truck.

"He ever take medicine?" Mick said.

"That stuff costs an arm and a leg."

"What about talking to somebody? Some kind of counselor maybe."

"He won't leave the bed to eat, let alone go to town. And them people, they don't make house calls."

"Does anybody anymore?"

"You do," Wade said.

Mick settled his gaze on Wade, opening himself to full interrogation mode, his vigilance like a net to capture any nuance.

"Do you know who might have hurt your aunt?"

Wade glanced around the yard nervously, then at the house.

"Well," he said, "it wasn't one of us."

"Somebody else then?"

"I don't know why you'd think I'd know that."

Mick nodded. Wade hadn't answered the question. That and his avoidance of eye contact communicated plenty. Lee Ann had done the same when he asked about a man in Nonnie's life.

"All right," Mick said. "I know it's tough on you'uns. See ya."

He drove out of the holler and toward town. The family's lies meant one thing—they knew who the killer was and wanted their own retribution. At the outskirts he stopped and took his phone from the glove box. There were three missed calls from his Commanding Officer in Germany, the last one included a voice mail. He ignored it, preferring not to hear Colonel Whitaker's flat reminder that Mick had overstayed his emergency family leave. He called his sister.

"It's me," he said. "I need to brief you. I ain't coming to your office."

"How about the jail?"

"Not my favorite place."

"You might want to this time," Linda said. "We got a man locked up for killing Nonnie."

"Did you charge him?"

"Yes and no. He's charged, but it wasn't us. The FBI brought him in. Something ain't right with this whole deal."

"All right. Give me a few minutes to eat."

"Half hour," Linda said and hung up.

He drove to a gas station with a sign that said CORN DOGS ON WEDNESDAY. Mick ate a can of Vienna sausages with saltines, the snack he'd missed the most overseas, and drank a bottle of Ale-8. It was Kentucky's only native soft-drink, entering the market after Coke, Pepsi, and Dr Pepper. The company's tardiness begat the name, A Late One, abbreviated to Ale-8-One. He bought a second bottle and a Twinkie, then drove to the jail.

Chapter Ten

The jail was closed, the stone walls bleaker than usual in the empty lot. Mick called Linda who informed him of the new jail's location where a tobacco warehouse had been. He arrived before she did. A Mercury entered the lot, a discontinued model, cheap in the hills because parts were scarce. It lacked a bumper. An older couple left the car, the woman carrying a sack, the man on a handmade cane. They walked past Mick with their heads down, ashamed of being seen visiting family.

Linda's SUV parked and she joined him. She looked sharp in her uniform and he wondered if she had several, or if she ironed the same one every night.

"What'd they need a new jail for?" he said.

"Drugs, mostly. Meth and Oxy. Heroin lately."

"Heroin?"

"Yeah. It's coming in from Detroit."

"When did this place open?" he said.

"Couple months ago. We had all the Frankfort politicians here for the ribbon cutting. They said it was the nicest
jail ever built."

"Old one overcrowded?"

"Oh, yeah. Cells were doubled up most of the time.
Weekends there'd be four men to a pod. Not enough room
to swing a cat."

"Then why shut it down? Looks like they'd use it for
drunks."

"Money," Linda said.

"Cost too much to run it?"

"No, they sold it for three million dollars. The college
is going to open a branch here."

Mick nodded. It was about like the state to start a
school in a building with no windows, no grounds, and no
private bathrooms. One of the local mandates was to edu-
cate ex-cons but he couldn't imagine anybody wanting to
take classes in the same building where they'd served time.

"Why are the Feds working your case?" he said.

"I don't know. It's one guy, temporarily assigned.
Johnny Boy can't stand him already."

"Who you got in jail?"

"The Dopted Boy."

"Tanner Curtis?"

She nodded.

For twelve years Tanner's parents had tried to get
pregnant, then adopted him from an agency in Lexington.

His arrival made the paper as the first adoption in county
history. Shy and quiet, Tanner was personally liked
but never accepted. In a culture that elevated blood
family above all, the community never trusted Tanner.
Throughout the county he was referred to as the "Dopted
Boy."

"On the phone," Mick said, "you said something wasn't
right."

"The FBI was here less than two days and brought him
in. The one guy nobody in the county cares about."

"What's Tanner say?"

"Nothing," she said. "Not word one. That's why I
want you to talk to him."

"All right. But I do it alone."

"I have to be in there or it's not official."

"That's the whole point."

"What do you mean?"

"Anything I find out," Mick said, "I'll tell you. Then
you can go in. Don't worry, he'll fold like a bobby pin."

"I don't like it."

A jet's contrail appeared above the nearest hill, slicing
a white line across the blue. It was too far for sound. Mick
wondered if animals noticed it, if birds were wary. The end
of the contrail began to disintegrate into ragged vapor that
drifted toward the lush green tree line.

"All right," she said. "Fuck it."

"That's the spirit, Sis."

They entered the jail and passed through security that included a full-body scan. A guard led them to an interrogation room where Linda gave Mick a final look of disapproval. He stepped inside and closed the door. The box was the same in every facility—designed to intimidate a suspect—small with stale air, a table screwed to the floor, a ringbolt in the table for cuffs, and two chairs. Though new, the room already smelled of sweat.

Tanner was in his mid-to-late twenties. His hair was trimmed to a style copied from TV—a slight side fade with a loose crop on top. His shirt was tucked in and his belt was shiny. Mick regarded his attire as the habit of an adored only child. He had the large features that photographed well—strong jaw, big eyes, and high cheekbones. His hands were cuffed.

Mick sat and offered the Ale-8 and snacks. Tanner reached for them then hesitated like a pup who feared he might be struck for violating rules he didn't know existed.

"It's all right," Mick said. "I done ate."

Mick left the room and found his sister watching a live video feed of the interrogation. A separate unit recorded audio playable in court. Reluctantly, she arranged for a guard to unlock Tanner's handcuffs. Mick returned and watched Tanner finish the Twinkie, then drink half the pop. He waited for the sugar and caffeine to hit, lifting Tanner's posture slightly, widening his eyes.

"I ain't law," Mick said. "Nothing you say to me goes anywhere."

In a slow, deliberate motion he pressed a button on the audio console to halt the recording. He leaned back and placed his hands behind his head, opening his body.

"Funny thing about Twinkies," Mick said. "They last longer than any other food. Up in Maine they got one that's forty-five years old."

"In the wrapper?" Tanner said.

"Nope, that's what I thought, too. It's just laying loose. They don't know what to do with it."

Tanner licked the cream filling from his fingers.

"You know why they got you in here, right?" Mick said. "It ain't good."

Tanner frowned then glanced at the wall-mounted video camera.

"That's for your protection," Mick said. "Keeps cops from getting out of hand. Don't worry, I ain't that way."

Tanner seemed anxious and wary, natural responses to incarceration. His expression held no defiance and his limbs were loose, not crossed in defense. Mick waited, watching for a nervous tic or hand gesture. Nothing about Tanner said he was a killer which meant he could be a sociopath or innocent. Or both. His eyes glittered with a buried intelligence, a trait Mick had as well. People in the hills learned early to conceal how smart they were.

"Tanner," he said. "Not talking makes you look guilty. It gives the impression you're hiding something. The cops think it's murder. Most people, in your situation, are pretty quick to deny it. Or they confess because they feel bad. But not talking is worse."

Tanner stared at the video camera mounted on the wall and shook his head. Mick stood and unbuttoned his shirt, revealing a T-shirt. He lifted it to show he wasn't wearing an audio wire then moved close to the camera. Staring into the lens, knowing his sister was watching, he removed his shirt and tossed it to drape the camera. He sat back at the table and let Tanner think about the offer of privacy for two minutes. Long enough for its meaning to sink in before he began wondering if it was a trick. Tanner lifted his hand to mimic talking on a phone.

"No cell phone," Mick said. "I don't like them."

Tanner's expression shifted to the disdain of disbelief. Mick stood and emptied his pockets—nothing but his wallet and a receipt for lunch.

"I keep it in the truck," Mick said. "Folks get mad if you don't answer and madder if you don't call back. Plus, there's some kind of etiquette about calling or texting that I can't figure out."

"You ever carry one?" Tanner said.

"Yeah, for work. Boss made me, but I'm not on the job no more."

"What was your work?"

"Army."

"You out?"

"Yes and no," Mick said. "Technically I'm six days

AWOL right now. I'd appreciate if you kept that to yourself."

Mick looked away quickly as if concerned that he'd said too much. The initial tension had eased. Mick had revealed personal information to establish rapport. Now they were two men occupying the same small space, not equals, but less distant than before. Due to the acoustic panels which amplified sound, Mick pitched his voice low and quiet.

"Three nights ago, a woman got killed on Choctaw. The FBI has made you for it. Those guys don't mess around. I can help you."

"Why?"

"Well, I guess I'm really helping my sister. She's the sheriff. She don't like the Feds trying to take over. Did you know Nonnie Johnson?"

"I knew who she was. I went to school with her kin."

"Were you up on Choctaw the other night?"

"No."

"Way it works, you need to tell me where you were."

"I can't. I won't."

"Okay," Mick said. "Then how about telling me why you can't. I'm sure there's a good reason."

"There is."

"You're a single man, right?"

Tanner nodded, squinting his eyes in a way Mick interpreted as increased wariness. The question had hit a vulnerable spot.

"Reason I ask," Mick said. "I don't care, really. But married women don't want their husbands to know if they were cheating. Is that what you were up to? Out tomcatting around with somebody's wife? The only thing you have to worry about is if she's married to the man you're talking to. But my wife, well, she might be pregnant by another fellow right now. So I reckon you're off the hook there."

"What?"

"I said, my wife is—"

"I heard you. Why are you telling me that?"

"Do you want the truth?" Mick said.

Tanner nodded.

"So you'll trust me," Mick said.

"That why you gave me food?"

"Partly. Plus I know what jail chow's like. Salty crap."

A long silence ensued during which Tanner stared into space and made a series of faces as he thought. Twice he began to speak then halted as if an invisible rope clamped his jaws shut. He shook his head. He fidgeted and popped his knuckles. When he sighed and leaned forward, Mick knew Tanner had convinced himself to talk.

Five minutes later Mick left the interrogation room. Linda met him in the hall, not quite bent out of shape, but well on the way. Her shoulders were so tense she could have been wearing pads beneath her uniform.

"Anything?" she said.

"Yeah."

"Best be worth it," she said. "I got the jailer up my butt like a rocket."

"Nice."

"Don't get smart. You in there alone, no recording. He's on his high horse with this new facility and protocol. Way he spoke got on my last nerve: 'pro-toe-call,' like a kid with a word he just learned."

"Let's get out of here," Mick said. "I got plenty to brief you on. And not in your office."

"I ain't going up to Papaw's cabin."

"Your house, then."

He walked away before she could argue, hearing her shout his name in exasperation. Outside he got in his truck and drove.

Chapter Eleven

Linda lived in the house she'd grown up in, having inherited it from their mother several years ago. It was in the middle of town at the dead end of Lyons Avenue. Mick parked on the street and waited. As a kid he went there occasionally but had always felt resentment emanating from his mother like a low-grade fever. Having no brothers and only married-in uncles, she regarded males as mysterious creatures who were loud and disruptive. Mick had confirmed all her beliefs. Her focus remained on Linda in the hopes that she would spurn family tradition, marry above her status, and move to Lexington. His sister had defied everything, disappointing her mother to an early grave.

Linda drove the SUV cruiser into the driveway and stopped before reaching the spindly carport. The vehicle was too wide to allow her to disembark easily. After navigating garbage cans, three rusty rakes, and a wheelbarrow with a flat tire, she opened the aluminum screen door and unlocked the wooden door to the kitchen. Mick followed her in. They'd always entered the house this way. The front was reserved for the preacher, formal company, and kids on Halloween.

The kitchen retained its original cabinetry—knotty pine with long, tapered hinges. The counters were formica, white with pale yellow boomerang shapes in an interlocking pattern. The old linoleum still lay on the floor, faded by footsteps in a path—sink, stove, refrigerator. A nail held a five-year-old calendar on top of several earlier calendars, a habit of their mother's. With age she'd developed a preoccupation with time—the house contained nine clocks, eleven calendars, and three egg timers. Outside each window was a thermometer, evidence of her other obsession. Mick recalled phone calls in which she'd periodically interrupt herself to relate an update on the time and temperature. He refrained from pointing out the obvious—what difference did either one make to a woman who hadn't left the house in four years?

He followed Linda into the front room. A gigantic smart TV dominated the space. The rest was unchanged— same ratty couch, easy chair, bulky end tables, and gigantic ugly lamps. Mick recalled driving a toy car along the perimeter of the rug. It was originally trimmed with white fringe but their mother had cut it off.

"I like what you've done here," he said, sprawling on the end of the couch.

"I figured I'd get married and sell it, or my husband would have furniture. Sometimes I don't think I have any home style."

"Sure you do. Mom's."

They laughed together, the years falling away. They could have been children giggling over a private joke.

"She was always so judgmental about other people's decor," Linda said. "'All their taste is in their mouth.' I heard her say that a thousand times."

"Mainly about people with stuff in their yards— flamingos, plastic sunflowers, and garden gnomes."

"But holiday decorations were okay. I didn't throw those out. Eleven boxes for Christmas, five for Easter, and twelve for everything else. Flag Day, Thanksgiving, and Fourth of July."

"What about Groundhog Day?" he said.

"You and your animals," she said. "How's that mule bite?"

"I should change the dressing, but it's all right."

A silence slid between them, broken by the ticking of numerous clocks. Mick wondered what his life might have been if his father had lived, if he'd grown up here. He'd probably run a car lot or manage the IGA and wind up resenting his entire life—job, town, wife, and his own thwarted ambition to get the hell out. Now he resented most of it anyway.

"Okay," she said. "What's the story on the Dopted Boy?"

"He's innocent."

"He told you that?"

"He's got an alibi. But he won't talk and neither will I. I'll tell you off the record only."

"This is not what I had in mind."

"You gave me a free hand."

"Is his alibi legal?"

"Yes," he said. "You're safe there."

"Can you verify the alibi?"

"Maybe. It'll take a little work."

She went to the kitchen, poured tap water into a pair of glasses, and brought them back. Mick's was frosted with a faded imprint of the state of Kentucky featuring notable landmarks. The only ones in the hills were Carter Caves and the Breaks of Big Sandy.

"Okay," Linda said. "We're off the record and I won't tell anyone. My word on it."

"The night Nonnie died, Tanner was in Lexington at a gay bar."

"What the fuck?"

"He left work early, went home, and took a shower. Changed clothes and drove up there. Sat outside for two hours getting his nerve up to go in. Stayed an hour and a half. Left and went to Arby's, then a gas station. Got home around midnight."

"You believe him?" she said. "I don't. Nothing gay about him."

"He didn't know for sure but thought he was. Tried Grindr twice. First time the guy didn't show. Second time he drove to Flemingsburg and got robbed. That was a year ago. Last Saturday he went to Lexington."

"Did he find out?"

"Not exactly. Not for sure anyhow. And that's why I believe him. The whole time, he felt like an outsider. They were Lexington people. Big city guys. He didn't belong and he knew it. He met three men and they snobbed him off. Said he felt worse than ever. Drove home depressed."

Mick drank half his glass of water.

"Here in Rocksalt," he said, "Tanner can't let anyone know who he is. Up there, he was excluded because he's from here. As an alibi, it's too personal to invent. Too painful to admit. I believe him."

"Maybe it wasn't Saturday night."

"I thought of that. He bought gas and Arby's with a credit card. Easy to check. But that's about all we can verify. No security cameras at the club. The staff won't talk about clients. If you think the cops' Blue Wall is tough, wait till you hit the Queer Wall. Bigger stakes."

"Fuck a duck," Linda said. "Fuck a big fat fucking downy duck."

Mick nodded, glancing around the room again. His mother's heavy drapes ran to the floor, topped by a thick valance that concealed the armature and rod. The room had always felt small, crowded by fabric.

"How'd you get all that?" Linda said.

"Interrogation 101. Food and drink, then my own secrets. You search his house?"

"Yes, not a damn thing. He's got a little narrow table just inside the door with six magazines on it. The top one was *Playboy*, then *Maxim*. Even a couple of old *Penthouses* on the bottom. I thought it was strange. Now it's just sad as hell."

"Could be worse," Mick said. "At least he's not living with his mother's clocks."

"Hardy-har-har. I took the cuckoo out of the cuckoo clock. Door opens and nothing comes out."

"Story of my life."

She laughed and he felt pleased with himself, like he was a kid entertaining her at the cabin. The old men didn't know how to talk to a girl, only give her things. Mick supposed he'd learned that, too. He'd married Peggy in part because she never asked for much. As a result he'd given her everything.

"I talked to Nonnie's family," he said. "They know more than they're letting on."

"Like what."

"Nonnie was mixed up with a man."

"They won't say who?"

"They won't even confirm that she was."

"But you think so."

"It was all over their faces. Classic obfuscation and displacement activity. No flat-out denials. I think they know who killed her. They're trying to get her boy to do something about it."

"Frankie?" she said. "He wouldn't hit a lick at a snake."

"I believe he's clinically depressed. He's more likely to shoot himself than anyone else."

"Where's that leave us?"

"You said old Mr. Tucker found the body?"

"Yeah," she said, "hunting ginseng."

"I'll go see him next."

"What about Fuckin' Barney?"

"Maybe he did it, maybe that's why he's hiding."

Linda stood and paced a tight little circle, a habit from childhood when frustrated. Mick knew that next she'd straighten something off-kilter, visible only to her. Sure enough, she adjusted the drapes, producing a cloud of dust that drifted to the floor.

"I guess I need to release Tanner," she said. "That'll piss off the FBI guy."

"Do you care?"

"Not really but maybe I should. That damn Murvil Knox is wanting to give me election money."

"Are you going to run?"

"I don't know. I like the job."

Mick nodded, wondering how they'd both wound up in law enforcement. No one else in their family ever had. Maybe it was a desire for order after their fractured childhood.

"Nice television set," Mick said. "You do anything else to the place?"

"Took down the pictures in the hall. I always thought it was weird, her putting all the family photos in the one part of the house that got no light."

Mick stood and glanced down the hallway. Despite the dimness, he could see a series of pale imprints where the pictures had hung for years. The wallpaper had yellowed around them. It was like looking at a gallery of ghosts.

He went through the kitchen to the side door. Linda followed.

"Something I need to tell you," she said.

Mick nodded, assuming it was about Peggy.

"I got a phone call," she said. "Said he was a garrison adjutant, whatever that is."

"Assistant to the commander."

"He wanted to know if I'd seen you. I told him you were in Germany. Hadn't been around here since winter."

"Good," he said.

"You in trouble?"

"Not yet."

"I can't see you committing any crime."

"My leave is up. That makes me AWOL."

"Because you're helping me?"

"No," he said. "It's Peggy, not you."

He left and Linda carried his empty glass to the kitchen. Her brother had always been secretive, but never toward family. His reticence about Peggy worried her. Linda could think of only one reason he was distraught and living at the cabin. She didn't want to consider the ramifications for their marriage.

Chapter Twelve

The car reeked of rancid fast food. Grease marks smeared the dashboard, and the steering wheel was slippery. Since noon Vernon and his partner had been parked on a scrap of earth at the bottom of a hill, the car obscured by a line of pines. They'd checked two other houses to confirm that their target was not staying with family. Now they were out in the damn woods. Vernon didn't like it. He was a city man. He liked streetlights, billboards, and pavement. Traffic exhaust was better than the stink of dirt wafting in the window. He needed better footwear than leather loafers and translucent socks. He craved conversation.

Previously Vernon partnered with a man who talked compulsively, expressing opinions on women, guns, sports, TV sets, automobiles, movies, and clothing. His adamantly delivered statements changed rapidly, contradicting themselves within minutes, each new one voiced with the same passion as the last. Vernon never had to talk. For nine hours on an interstate drive, his former partner had once debated which was better—Arby's, McDonalds, Burger King, Taco

Bell, or KFC. The guy essentially argued with himself, pointing out attributes and flaws until reaching a five-way draw. Vernon had grunted in agreement. Two minutes later the guy cursed and said he'd forgotten all about Chipotle!

His new partner, Freddie, rarely spoke, communicating with single words such as "smokes," or "piss," or "food." Mainly he twirled a pocketknife like a miniature baton between his fingers. Vernon began wondering if his silence meant he might snap any minute and gut him like a hog right there in the car seat. That led to speculating which side of the car was safest. Sitting behind the steering wheel offered more protection. At the very least Freddie would require a more precise aim of the blade. Vernon had taken to leaning forward, practically hunched over the steering wheel. His lower back ached. Worse, he was starting to feel foolish. He was cold and bored, and to top it off he had a silent seatmate.

"What do we know about this guy?" Vernon said.

Freddie stared through the window for a few minutes.

"Drunk," he finally said.

"Not living with his wife," Vernon said. "That might mean something."

Freddie shrugged. Great, Vernon thought.

From outside came a fierce sound of rattling leaves. Vernon's hand instinctively moved to his pistol. He considered what he knew about bears—don't shoot them in the head, the bullet will bounce off. Run downhill because bears can't. If cornered, climb a tree that's too fragile for the bear but how would he know which tree couldn't hold a bear? The noise became louder as the bear got closer. He considered rolling the window up then decided he needed it open to shoot. Freddie shifted beside him, staring out the window, knife in one hand, gun in the other. The sound was very near, a fearsome clatter like a series of detonations as the animal approached. Vernon withdrew his pistol, his heart beating hard, his vision scanning the trees. A squirrel scampered through the dead leaves of the forest floor then jumped to a young hickory. The noise stopped. Both men tucked their weapons away.

"Look, man," Vernon said. "Last guy I worked with, he ran his mouth nonstop. Drove me crazy but at least it filled time. You and me, we need to talk. No sense getting jittery over a squirrel."

"That guy," Freddie said. "Tall and skinny but slow moving? Went by Cool Dick?"

"Yeah."

"He's dead."

"On the job?"

"I heard it was over a woman. Only guy I worked with was him."

"Same here," Vernon said. "They must have put him with quiet guys. Smart. But now we're partnered up. We got to talk. I'm hearing bears over here."

"He ever go on about fast food?"

"For hours, dude."

"Same here," Freddie said. "One thing he said stuck with me."

"What's that?"

"You never hear of Italian fast food."

"Fazoli's."

"Italian, yes. Fast, no. You have to wait."

"What's the cutoff for fast?" Vernon said. "Two minutes? Three?"

"If it has a drive-thru."

"Good point."

Vernon leaned away from the steering wheel, satisfied that his new partner had no intention to stab him. The work bred paranoia, a kind of emotional collateral damage that it was best to acknowledge and ignore. He watched the dirt road, hoping the target showed up before dark. The woods scared him at night. He figured that was why so many movies were about scary stuff in the woods—witches, haunted houses, ghosts, and monsters.

"You like movies?" he said.

Freddie shrugged.

"I do," Vernon said. "My favorite are aliens from outer space."

"Like E.T.?"

"No, dude. The kind that attack a spaceship. What kind do you like?"

"Rom-coms."

"You're shitting me."

"Women like them. If you try and like what women like, you get more women."

Vernon regretted the subject. At least with Cool Dick he'd have a decent conversation about movies. He tried to think of something else to discuss.

Chapter Thirteen

Mick left his sister's house and headed east. The sun lay above the hillside as if resting, tinging the western treetops with flame. He followed the blacktop deeper into the hills before turning onto a dirt lane and climbing a steep slope that was more rain gully than road. He made a sharp curve to a ridge that ended at a house surrounded by heavy woods. There was more sun here and he briefly pitied people who lived in the hollers where it was already night.

He waited in the truck and watched for dogs. People unaccustomed to visitors in an unknown vehicle were capable of greeting a stranger with a weapon. He drove a little closer and gunned the engine in case the old guy was going deaf. In grade school the janitor never talked much but was always present, stoking the big furnace with coal in winter, cleaning one classroom per day, repairing any problems with plumbing. He was kind and soft-spoken, and Mick figured he would be still. He'd noticed that men softened as they aged, whereas women tended to toughen up.

A male cardinal gave its cry to draw attention while the rust-colored female flew a low, straight line toward a blackberry thicket. She was trying to fool Mick by leading him away from her nest. The screen door opened and the janitor stepped onto the porch. Mick was surprised to see how small he was, not much over five feet tall. He stood at an angle to the edge of the porch with one hand out of sight behind his body. Mick figured he was armed. He rolled the truck window down and leaned out.

"Hidy, Mr. Tucker, I knowed you in grade school. I'm Mick Hardin. You got time to talk a minute?"

"Ain't you got a boy looks a lot like you?"

"I am that boy."

"Jimmy your daddy?"

"Yeah, and my granddaddy was Homer Jack."

"All right, then."

Tucker nodded and Mick left the truck. He walked to the edge of the oak steps and stopped. A breeze carried sassafras and Mick recalled his grandfather chewing its twigs like candy. The leaves were soft as suede.

"I'm here about that woman up on Choctaw."

"You law?" Tucker said.

"No."

"Kin to the dead woman?"

"No."

"Ain't no other reason for you to be up here."

"My sister's the sheriff."

"I heard about her," Tucker said. "Ain't you in the army?"

"Iraq and Afghanistan. Syria till the withdrawal."

"Infantry?"

"At first. Then Airborne. Lately CID."

"Reckon you'll re-up, time comes?"

"Maybe," Mick said.

"I thought about it my ownself."

"You served?"

"Korea. 108th Airborne."

"Tough war."

"Reckon they all are if you're in it," Tucker said. "Come up on the porch and set."

Mick climbed the steps and sat in a wicker chair with holes in the back. The cushion was fluffy as a cat. Tucker took a rocking chair but didn't rock. His eyes were different colors and Mick recalled his buddies talking about that in grade school. Somebody had said he was part goat.

"I'm not official," Mick said. "Helping my sister is all. She said you found the body."

"She looked a Turner."

"She was. Married a Johnson."

"Out of that bunch from Lower Lick Fork Creek that moved to town?"

"Might be," Mick said. "I don't know the family history."

The air stilled and a distant dove moaned, the sound traveling through the trees. The house sat on a wedge of land at the end of the ridge, as isolated as his grandfather's cabin, but a prettier spot. The grass stopped at the hillside, bordered by a row of iris and forsythia. Two yard oaks shaded the front and would allow winter sun to heat the porch.

"You remember what time you found her?" Mick said. "I'm trying to figure out when she died."

"I was hunting sang."

"Uh-huh."

The old man was staring at him as if waiting for Mick to go on.

"Did you not have a watch on you?" Mick said.

"I was hunting sang."

"Yes sir, I understand that."

"It grows on eastern hillsides. Shady and cool."

Tucker nodded. His face held an expression of expectation, and Mick recalled him being taciturn to the point of mysterious in grade school. Then he figured out what the old man meant.

"You were there early," Mick said, "to see the plants good."

"About a half hour after sunup. Any earlier and it's too dark. Sun's got to get high enough over the hill to hit the bottom of the slope. Wait too long and you can't see them for the shade."

Tucker was the same generation as Mick's grandfather with all the complicated contradictions of the old culture deep in the hills. Forthright but not forthcoming. Honest but reticent. Watchful but friendly.

"I used to visit you in the boiler room at school," Mick said.

"A few of you boys did."

"It was peaceful in there."

"What it was, was warm. You fellers came in there on cold days during lunch break."

"You showed me how to whittle a belt balancer."

The old man nodded, his eyes crinkling in a smile that never made it to his mouth.

"How's your belt?" Tucker said.

"Balanced out."

"You don't want your belt getting curled up like a honey locust seed pod."

"No sir," Mick said. "That's no damn good."

"My wife is in the house."

"Sorry, Mr. Tucker. I won't cuss no more. You see anybody else on Choctaw?"

"No."

"Hear ary a car?"

"No."

"If that's your spot, I figure you check on the sang every now and again."

Tucker stared at him. Time and age had drooped skin over the outside edges of each eyesocket, partially obscuring the irises. To reduce any perceived threat, Mick focused his left eye on Tucker's right. It was a tactic of interrogation and he'd been surprised how well it worked. If the subject became confused or anxious, he switched focus—left eye to left eye—which worked as a kind of reset. Tucker wasn't hiding anything, but was waiting for a question, the sign of a smart and patient man.

"Did you ever see anyone up on Choctaw other times?" Mick said.

"Yep."

"You know who they were?"

"Yep."

"Would you mind telling me who?"

"That woman and some younger feller."

"Did you know him?"

"Just saw his back."

"Remember what he looked like?"

"Dark-headed. Flannel shirt. Dungarees."

"What about size?"

"Can't rightly say. I was looking downhill at him."

Mick nodded and stared off into the woods. A squirrel chittered from a tree, warning a blue jay that held its ground. The squirrel sprang away and the bird continued about its business.

"What do you think that squirrel's up to?" Mick said.

"Getting acorns."

"Him and that bird feuding over nuts?"

"They're there every day," Tucker said. "I tried to make a pet of one or the other. Ain't had no luck. Squirrel's too dumb for it. And the jaybird's too smart."

A rustle came from in the house, then a light thump and a cough. Tucker stood.

"My wife," he said. "She's poorly."

"I thank you for your time."

Mick rose and walked to his truck. He lifted his hand in farewell then drove off the hill, wondering where dogs and cats fit into Tucker's animal philosophy. Dogs were loyal and cats were survivors. Mick figured he was a little of both. Otherwise there was no reason for him to stay in Kentucky and put his career at risk.

Chapter Fourteen

The air outside Vernon's car was utterly black, no ambient illumination, no brightly lit signs, no streetlights or lurid neon inviting him to a tavern. What the fuck did these people do out here at night? Sleep? The sound of a vehicle came along the road, startling in the silence. He watched an old truck trundle by, headed up the hill. The air was too dark to match the driver's face to the photograph, but the truck fit the description and who the hell else would be wandering around out here but the target?

Vernon waited five minutes then drove up the road with the headlights off. At the top of the hill he stopped.

"He might be tough," Vernon said. "Army trained and all that."

"Those guys are shit without somebody giving them orders. I'll take the back door."

"I want the back. I'm bored."

"I called it," Freddie said.

"You want to rock-paper-scissor it?"

"Fuck you. Bust that light out."

Freddie left the car. Vernon used the barrel of his pistol to break the interior light. Red plastic chips fell to the dashboard. He pulled the key partway from the ignition, just far enough so the alarm wouldn't beep, but still inserted for a quick getaway, a trick he'd learned years ago. He departed the vehicle and left the door open. Gun in hand he walked beside the road, staying in the deep shadows, unaware that the sound of his shoes and splay-footed urban strut gave his position away.

Mick had seen the car tucked behind the pines and wondered if his commanding officer had sent it. Such a move was unorthodox but the colonel was prone to playing loose. It was one of the reasons Mick liked working for him. Dispatching men to bring him home and avoid an AWOL charge was smart. Whoever they were, they couldn't negotiate the darkness of the woods, raising a racket like a couple of children. Two men meant one would cover each door.

Mick went to their car and removed the key. He made a wide loop around the house, out the ridge, down a slope, then climbed it to approach the rear of the cabin. He moved silently and easily until he could see the man peering in the back door. The dumb son-of-a-bitch was using his cell phone as a flashlight. The other hand held a 9mm pistol. Mick moved closer. He breathed through his nose to avoid hearing the sound of his own breath in the miniature echo chamber of his mouth. Nothing existed, not the woods, the night, the cabin, or himself. The man was the focus. Mick held his breath as he moved directly behind him.

"Hey," he said.

Startled, the man jumped and spun. Mick flung his right forearm at the man's face, hitting him in the temple with the edge of his elbow. The man fell backward as if sawn off at the ankles. Mick caught him with both arms and eased him to the ground. He took the man's cell phone, pistol, wallet, and pocketknife. Working swiftly, he cut several strands of Virginia creeper off the wall of the house and hog-tied the man. Then he sliced off a part of his shirt, stuffed it in his mouth and secured it with more vine. If the man was allergic, too bad, he shouldn't be out in the woods.

The intruder at the front might have heard the noise and Mick listened intently for three minutes, hearing the persistent buzz of cicadas, a barred owl proclaiming its turf, and the auk-auk of a nighthawk. He entered the woods and circled the house. From the heavy shade of the old smoke-house he watched a man in a leather jacket attempting to hide behind an oak in the yard. The half-moon brightened the night enough to give the tree a dark shadow in the grass with the form of a man at the base. These were street-meat, junior tough guys with as much sense as God gave a goose. Mick could have taken them out with a slingshot.

He tossed a rock against the cabin's window. The man ducked, a response that amused Mick. Why duck when you're hiding behind a tree? The man pressed a button on his cell phone, causing Mick's pocket to vibrate. He waited until it went to voice mail, then returned the call, and began walking toward the tree. The man quickly answered the phone, whispering hello. Standing directly behind him, Mick said, "Hidy." The man turned his head and Mick clipped him in the temple with his gun barrel. He blinked twice and took a step. Mick struck him again and he dropped.

Mick disarmed him and went in the house for rope. He tied the man's wrists together in front of him, then lashed him tightly to the oak. He carried the other man to the front, cut the vines, and tied him the same as the first man. They were in a sitting position, backs to the tree as if the oak had flourished from between their bodies. Two of their legs were lashed together, their thighs, knees, and ankles touching. Mick passed a final rope against their throats, snug but not too tight. If either one moved, they'd both feel it cutting into their windpipe.

Inside he drank two glasses of water, sweating from adrenaline and exertion. With a flashlight he sat on the gray steps to the porch, examining the men's pocket litter. Detroit driver's licenses. One credit card each. Four hundred and sixty dollars between them. A photograph of him, an old one pulled off a military website. His face was thinner. The collar of his shirt was askew, revealing a sharp tan line. He'd been a gung-ho soldier for his first tour, less so on his second due to the waste of resources and manpower. Too many dead comrades. Too many betrayals by local contacts. Transferring to MP had reignited his enthusiasm, which was solidified by promotion to CID.

One of his prisoners stirred. Mick carried a dipper of water from the cistern and poured it over their heads. He leaned down and smacked each in the face, open-handed. Both men sputtered, eyes blinking first from the water then the harsh beam of the flashlight. They slowly became aware of their restraints. Mick watched the sense of failure descend upon them, followed by frustration and anger.

"That's a bug bath," Mick said. "Rain barrel gets full of insects. Dead though, so they won't bite. You're safe on that score."

"Fuck you," said the back-door man.

"You're Frederick Clarence Kornspudt," Mick said. "Bet you got called Cornhole as a kid. Made you tough, right? How tough are you? We'll find out."

Mick shifted the flashlight to the other man.

"And you are Vernon V. Armstrong, Junior. Don't tell me, the 'V' is for Vernon."

"Victor," Vernon said.

"I knew some Armstrongs growing up. You got people down here?"

Vernon shrugged.

"You must be from that bunch that went north to work them car factories. Reckon it didn't suit you. Too bad. Punching the clock might be better than out here tied to a tree like a dog."

"What do you want?" Vernon said.

"There it is," Mick said. "The top question. Seeing as how you're tied up and I ain't, I'm the one who gets to do the asking. So tell me, Vernon, what do you want?"

From the creek came a cacophony of small frogs that was temporarily silenced by the massive croak of a bullfrog. A slice of the Milky Way was visible like froth above the tree line.

"All right," Mick said. "Nobody's talking. You boys are hard as walnuts. Here's what I know—somebody sent you here. What I don't know is who and why. You can tell me or you can sleep out here and we'll start fresh in the morning."

Neither man spoke. Mick stood and walked toward them.

"Okay, sleepy time it is. I need to tie you tighter but I'm out of rope. Bungee cords will work. They might cut off some circulation. Not to worry, I'm an early riser. Your legs won't get gangrene."

He cut the flashlight and spoke into the darkness.

"Atrophy of the limbs won't really matter because this is wildcat country. The females are in heat so the males are out chasing after them. You know how it is. They can't help themselves. They'll find you before the bungee cords do any serious nerve damage."

He climbed the steps and entered the house, making sure the screen door slammed hard. He grinned to himself. Wildcats avoided people except during August when they followed dry creek beds down to the hollers for water. These two Detroit idiots wouldn't know that. He could hear them whispering in the yard and made a mental bet with himself that they'd respond within two minutes. Instead, one of the men called out at the forty-second mark.

"We'll talk," he said. "But you have to let us go."

"No deal," Mick said.

He heard another huddled conversation.

"What do you want to know?" the man yelled.

Mick stepped outside, flicked the flashlight on and aimed it at the men. From the stacked woodpile he hefted a chunk of oak kindling. Knives scared people more than guns, but a club was the most menacing. He assumed it was the vestige of some primitive memory, Neanderthal fear. A burning torch was the most terrifying weapon but it would take too long to assemble.

"Who sent you?" he said.

"Charley Flowers," Vernon said.

"Who's he?"

"Our boss."

Mick struck Freddie's shin with the oak stick. He yelped and tried to scramble out of range but was held by the ropes tied to the other man. Another trick Mick learned in the desert—the jolt of impact traveled to the second man's leg and he'd imagine the pain as his own. Freddie subsided his writhing and Mick hit him again, harder.

"Charley Flowers," Mick said.

"He runs smack from Detroit to the hills," Vernon said.

"What's that got to do with me?"

Vernon was silent and Mick struck Freddie again, closer to his knee.

"What the fuck, man," Freddie said. "I ain't said nothing."

"That's why."

Mick lightly tapped Freddie's knee twice, then drew back the stick for a hard blow.

"Wait," Freddie said. "Don't."

"Talk to me."

"Fuckin' Barney is Charley's main man down here. Every two weeks he meets a driver at the rest stop on I-64 and gets the product."

"Which rest stop?"

"The one closest to Rocksalt."

"Why send you after me?"

"Charley heard you were looking for Fuckin' Barney. Didn't know who you were, DEA or a new player. He sent us to find out."

"And do what?"

"If you were a Fed, we were supposed go back home."

"And if I ain't," Mick said.

"Give you a warning to leave Fuckin' Barney alone."

"Anything else?"

"That's everything."

"It's never everything," Mick said. "How'd you know about this place up here?"

"Charley told us."

The air cooled sharply and the night sounds ceased. A storm was coming, a sudden wind, then lightning and rain. A good night to drink bourbon under the oak and listen to a thousand drops of water slap a thousand leaves around him. He couldn't, not tonight. He had too much to do. He could turn his prisoners over to Linda but they hadn't committed a crime. If they were ex-cons, she could charge them with possession of a firearm. Too much paperwork for no gain.

"How's your leg?" he said.

"Hurts," Freddie said.

"I don't care about Charley Flowers or his drug business. I need to talk to Fuckin' Barney. Look at it this way. The law on the hunt for him messes with your all's business. You help me talk to him and things go back the way they were."

"What about us?" Freddie said.

"You go home to Detroit."

"I don't know," Vernon said. "Fuckin' Barney won't like it."

"So what," Mick said. "You're the Motor City muscle. What you say goes. Or you can tell Mr. Flowers exactly what happened up here tonight. I'll give you a couple of minor gunshot wounds to make it real enough for him to believe it. The nuns got a hospital in Rocksalt but that'll draw attention you don't want. Problem is, it's a long drive

back to Detroit bleeding and shot. But don't worry if that's
what you want. One shot apiece, a through-and-through,
nothing vital, no arteries hit. I'll bandage your wounds.
What's it going to be?"

"We don't know where he is," Vernon said.

"Who told your boss I was looking for him?"

"Fuckin' Barney's mother."

Mick laughed. The old lady had fooled him good.

"I'm hungry," he said. "You boys hungry? Let's eat
then go visit Mrs. Kissick."

In the house Mick unloaded the men's guns, opened
three cans of SpaghettiOs, and carried them outside. He
cut the ropes binding their wrists. Mick ate with a fork and
gave them spoons.

"Man," Vernon said, "I love SpaghettiOs. It's all I ate
as a kid, you know. It's better warm, though. This how you
eat out here all the time, cans and spoons. Some kind of
outdoorsy thing?"

"No," Mick said. "I don't trust you with a fork."

"You can gouge out a man's eye with a spoon."

"Shut up," Freddie said. "I'm trying to eat."

Mick gave them water then rolled up Freddie's pants
leg. The thin fabric moved easily to his knee, revealing
three red welts.

"Didn't break the skin," Mick said. "It'll bruise but
you can walk. We'll take your car."

The men nodded. Mick cut the ropes and herded them
to the car with his gun.

"Vernon drives," Mick said. "Freddie, you're in the front, too. I'll be in the back. Anything gets hinky, I'll shoot through the car seats to muffle the sound. Got it?"

Once situated in the vehicle, Mick produced the keys which surprised both men. Freddie glanced at Vernon and shook his head in contempt.

Chapter Fifteen

They drove silently off the hill to the blacktop then used back roads to get to the Kissick house. The porch light came on and a man stepped out with a rifle. Mick grinned—it was the worst weapon for the situation, unsuitable for close quarters. He rolled his window down.

"It's Mick Hardin," he said. "You Mrs. Kissick's boy?"

"Yeah," the man said. "I'm Mason."

"Need to talk to your mom a minute."

"She done went to bed."

"Get her," Mick said. "Tell her it's business. I've got two boys from Detroit with me."

"She don't like getting waked up."

"Better you do it than I start honking the horn, then tell her it's on account of you. Now get to it. Won't take long."

Mason stood motionless for twenty seconds, a child's version of defiance, then entered the house. A few minutes later he came out, shoulders slumped with chagrin.

"She said you can come in. But not them."

"Nope," Mick said. "I can't leave them on their own. They might take off."

"Can you not handcuff them or something?"

"You got ary a set?"

Mason shook his head.

"Me, neither," Mick said. "I'm getting out but I'm staying right here. Go on and get her."

The man nodded and went in the house again.

"Give me the keys," Mick said to Vernon. "Then roll your window down. A one of you leaves this vehicle, I'll cut you down like straw."

He left the car and stood far enough from the window that Vernon couldn't reach him. A half-moon had risen, suspended in the sky like a broken plate, dousing light from nearby stars. A female barred owl began her high-pitched babble followed by the calls of two males vying for her favor.

Shifty Kissick stepped onto the porch in a long flannel robe over a nightgown and slippers. One side of the robe sagged from what he figured was the weight of a sidearm. He'd underestimated her once but wouldn't again. Mason stood beside her with the rifle.

"Mrs. Kissick," he said. "I'm sorry for getting you up."

"What are you wanting?"

"These Detroit boys tried to get the drop on me."

She peered into the dark car.

"I don't know them," she said.

"I don't, either. I'm game to let them go and forget what they told me."

"About what?"

"Your all's family business. Heroin. Charley Flowers. All that."

"You can't trust a word they say."

"Charley Flowers sent them down here to warn me off hunting for your son."

"I can see how good that went."

"Ma'am, I think you know where your son is. Let me talk to him and I'll send these boys home. If I have to kill them, Mr. Flowers will have two options. One, he sends men meaner than them. Or, two, he'll cut his losses and run smack to somebody else besides you."

"You'd make an enemy of me. Of all the Kissicks."

"I can see that, ma'am. But I'll be back overseas. Worst that could happen is I can't come home no more, which ain't that bad considering how this visit's been shaping up."

"You got a wife hereabouts," she said.

"Let me speak a little plainer, Mrs. Kissick. I've never threatened your family and I'd appreciate if you gave me the same courtesy."

She nodded.

"Thank you," he said. "After I talk to your boy, you won't see me again."

"He ain't here."

"Would you mind calling him. Won't take but a minute."

"What do you want from him?" she said.

"Who he saw on Choctaw. What time. The kind of car they were in."

"He won't like it."

"Ma'am, you don't like getting woke up. I don't like having these Detroit boys in the car. The fact is, none of us likes any of this. So if you get him on the phone, we can quit the not-liking and get some sleep."

In the dim light of the porch her face showed nothing, which impressed him. Briefly he wondered how he'd have turned out with her as a mother instead of a shut-in who collected clocks. He'd be moving dope through the hills and Fuckin' Barney would be in the army.

"Phone," she said to Mason.

He handed her a cell phone. She pressed a single button and after a few seconds began talking too quietly for Mick to hear. If things went sideways, he'd give her a leg wound while Mason was lifting the rifle. Seeing his mother hurt would rattle him and Mick could pick him off easily.

She passed the phone to her son who brought it down the three steps and across the yard. Mick moved toward the rear of the car.

"Just set it on the hood," he said.

Mason glanced at his mother who gave a quick nod, and he did as he'd been told.

"Mason," he said, "I need a little favor. How about you aim your rifle at these boys in the car while I'm talking to your brother."

Again he looked to his mother for approval of the request. She nodded and Mick picked up the phone. The contact name said "F.B." Mick held it to his ear.

"You're a hard man to find," he said.

"I ain't wanting to be found."

"I know you were up on Choctaw the night Nonnie Johnson got killed. I want to know who all was up there."

"I ain't telling you nothing."

"I ain't the law," Mick said.

"It ain't the law I'm worried about."

Mick cocked his head, thinking rapidly. Whatever Fuckin' Barney knew had caused him to hole up. He was afraid of somebody.

"Who are you hiding from?" Mick said.

"Are you deaf? I ain't saying nothing. Only reason I'm talking is Mommy asked me to."

"I understand that," Mick said. "You're loyal to your mother."

"Damn right."

"I've got two boys from Detroit here."

"Mommy done told me."

"Listen at me a minute, will you? I can call my sister right now. She'll bring the State Police and the FBI. They'll hear all about Charley Flowers and how you're selling smack for him. They'll lock everyone of y'all up, your mom, too. You don't want the Detroit mob on your ass. And you're too good a son to let your mom go to jail for you. So how about you tell me what I want to know."

"You're a fucking prick."

"I've heard that a thousand times. Tell me something I don't know. Who killed Nonnie? Who are you hiding from?"

Fuckin' Barney talked for two minutes. Mick ended the call and waved Mason back toward the house. He tossed the phone in the yard and nodded to Mrs. Kissick.

"Thank you, ma'am," he said. "One more thing."

"Ain't that ever the way of it," she said.

"Don't tell nobody else where my papaw's place is. It'll go a whole lot rougher next time."

"You're your father's son, all right," she said. "You know he courted me right here about forty years ago."

"You didn't like him?"

"Oh, I did. But he was bad to be wild back then."

"I've heard that," Mick said. "See ya."

He got in the back seat, gave Vernon the keys, and told him to drive back to the cabin. He ordered them to sit under the tree, which they did with swift obedience. It was another interrogation tactic, one he'd derived from learning about the training of young elephants. They were chained to a stake for the first few years of their lives. When the chains were removed, the trainer drove a stake in the ground and the elephants stayed close to it.

While Vernon and Freddie sat, he searched the car carefully, finding nothing.

"All right," he said. "You two can go."

"What're you looking for?" Vernon said.

"Spare ammunition."

He returned their unloaded pistols.

"Sorry about the leg," he said.

"Don't hurt much," Freddie said, shrugging. "Can I have my knife, too?"

"You can get that kind anywhere," Mick said.

"My uncle gave it to me."

Mick tossed it to him.

"Thanks," Freddie said.

Mick nodded. The men got in the car.

"You can tell Charley Flowers ever what you want," Mick said. "But let him know I ain't interested in him. Anybody else comes sniffing around my house and I will be."

Vernon drove away. Mick watched the taillights until they faded in the darkness. He could hear them going down the hill in first gear, the engine straining against the pull of gravity. When the sound dissipated he went into the cabin.

At the foot of the hill Vernon stopped at the blacktop. The car smelled worse now. Fear-sweat always did but it was the first time he'd smelled his own. Freddie lit a cigarette and stepped out of the car, stretching his leg and putting weight on it. Vernon joined him.

"How is it?" he said.

"Not bad," Freddie said. "Your family really from here?"

"Yeah. They moved up to Detroit in the eighties."

"You should be glad they left," Freddie said. "What the fuck kind of place is this place?"

"Daddy told me it was the last National Forest the government made. The town was already here."

"These people really are living in the goddam woods." Freddie laughed, a rarity in itself. The sound was coarse as if rusty from disuse. "Let's get out of here."

"Thought I might visit my cousins."

"Why?" Freddie said.

"Get more ammo."

"He took us down like we were fish," Freddie said. "I ain't going at him without more crew. Fuck that guy and fuck this place."

"What about Charley?"

"We tell him Hardin ain't a player or a Fed. We warned him off. Job done."

"That old lady knows what happened."

"She ain't the talking type."

"What if she is?" Vernon said. "Charley won't like it."

"Then what, we stay down here and pop them all? Hardin, Fuckin' Barney, the old lady, and whoever else is in that house. That your plan?"

"Maybe my cousins'll help."

"Cousins you ain't never met. Fat fucking chance."

"What's your plan, then?" Vernon said.

"Go home and get paid. Smoke on the weed for a week. Wait for the next job."

Vernon studied the heavy woods that surrounded them, the shadowed land, the narrow strip of stars visible between the hills. He didn't want to stay here, either. His pride wasn't worth the risk of further humiliation.

"All right," he said. "We'll stop in Dayton and eat."

In the cabin Mick lay on his back, pistol at hand, staring at the dim ceiling illuminated by a scrap of moon. He figured those two city boys wouldn't bother him again. They'd started at the bottom, moved up to working for a big boss, and were unaware that they'd already topped out. Their confidence and energy had helped them as younger men, but they would advance no further. They weren't smart enough, bold enough, or tough enough. Guys like them wound up dead or serving time.

Chapter Sixteen

Mick awoke at seven o'clock, swiftly alert, listening to a yellow-breasted warbler sing from the understory beyond his window. The sky was pale blue, etched by a strip of red above the tree line. After changing the bandage on his mule bite, he armed himself and drove off the hillside, halting at a wide spot in the road. He dug his cell phone out of the glove box and checked his phone log—two more from Germany, which he ignored. He texted Linda to meet him at the Smokey Valley Truck Stop for breakfast. She responded immediately:

> closed 5 years ago dumshit. meet at bob's
> i-64 connector. 20 mins

He drove to Bob's, a gas station that sold milk, eggs, cigarettes, and fishing tackle. A shelf held a row of orange life-preservers inside plastic bags covered in dust, evidence that people in the hills were less concerned with drowning

than spending money. As his grandfather said, people who
can't swim should stay off a lake. The back area had a steam
table emitting the strong smell of sausage. Four older men
sat in a corner with coffee, stridently debating the chances
of the Cincinnati Reds. Linda was a few minutes late, her
hair still damp from a shower.

"You eat?" she said.

He shook his head and they moved to the counter.
A skinny woman with a nose ring filled cardboard plates
with scrambled eggs, sausage, biscuits, gravy, and discs of
blackened potatoes. Linda adjusted her equipment belt to
sit in the small chair. She loaded a fork with a fragment of
each food, then spoke.

"What's so important you had to meet this early?"

"Not here."

"I forgot what a cranky bastard you are in the morning. Hungover?"

"No, I quit," Mick said. "You don't have to worry I'm
like Dad."

"Fuck you."

"And I'm cranky?"

He ate as he'd been taught, one hand holding the
biscuit. His grandfather called it a "pusher," and Mick
recalled him saying "Reach me another pusher." They
finished eating and walked to Linda's vehicle. Sunlight
seeped across the pocked lot, illuminating oil stains in
rainbows of dew.

"You still got Tanner Curtis locked up?" he said.

"No, I cut him loose last night. You'd know that if you bothered to stay in touch. You'd also know I got another call from Germany. They know you're here."

"I was due back last week."

"Trouble?"

"My CO will cover for me. Worst that can happen is I'll get an Article 15. No penalty, but they can mandate psychological counseling."

"I pity that poor doc if you show up."

"Won't happen," Mick said. "It's for people with emotional problems or substance abuse. Something that made them go AWOL. They know I'm coming back."

"Then why's he keep calling?"

"I don't know. But I'm not leaving till I see Peggy, which is not something I want to talk about."

"Okay, big bro. What do you want to talk about?"

"I know who killed Nonnie."

Linda's face closed down, hardening with acute intensity. She opened the door and climbed into the cab. Mick went to the other side and got in.

"When did you find out?" she said.

"Last night."

"Why didn't you tell me then?"

"There were some complications. By the time I took care of them, it was late and I was tired."

"I've never known you to be tired your whole life."

"The complications were pretty damn complicated. Point is, I know the identity of the killer. Delmer Collins."

"You sure?" she said.

"I talked to Fuckin' Barney. He was up on Choctaw that night. Delmer saw him when he was leaving. The next day Fuckin' Barney got a little visit from a man who threatened him. That's why he's hiding out. It's not the law he's scared of, it's Delmer's uncle. Murvil Knox."

"That son of a bitch," she said. "That's why Knox put the FBI in my office. He arrested the Dopted Boy to steer things away from his nephew."

She pounded the steering wheel three times, looked at her fist, then shook her hand as if flinging water off.

"Where's Delmer at?" she said.

"Finding out is my next plan."

"I need to see Fuckin' Barney."

"Can't do it," he said. "I agreed to leave him out if he told me what he knew."

"Leave him out of what?"

"He's moving heroin in. They make the exchange at the Eldridge County rest stop on the interstate."

"Let me get this straight. You got a drug-dealer witness who won't come forward because he's afraid. You don't know where the killer is or why he did it. And I've got a guy reporting every move I make to the killer's uncle."

"About the size of it," Mick said.

"I got to sidetrack the FBI guy."

Mick nodded.

"I can call their field office in Louisville," Linda said. "Tell them I've got intel on a heroin ring and don't have the manpower to monitor it. I'll request Special Agent Wilson for surveillance at the rest stop."

"Think they'll listen?"

"I'll tell them any arrests are theirs, not mine."

"That's a good plan, Sis," Mick said. "Smart."

"Did Fuckin' Barney tell you about the rest stop?"

"No, I got that info another way."

"One of your complications?"

He nodded, thinking about Vernon and Freddie. They were probably still asleep after driving all night. He kind of half-liked them, overgrown boys similar to hundreds he'd met on bases in Europe.

"Anything else?" she said.

"My gut says Delmer is still yet around here. His uncle will keep him close for control. Whatever you do, don't let Knox know you're looking at Delmer. His muscle scared Fuckin' Barney and that family doesn't strike me as scaring easy."

"Oh, you know the whole family now?"

"Dad went out with the mother before he married Mom."

"This don't get no better."

"It could get a lot worse if Knox finds out what we know."

She gathered breath again. Mick figured her hand still ached or she'd be pounding the steering wheel again.

"What are you going to do?" she said.

"I'm going to go talk to Old Man Tucker again. He lived all his life in these hills. If there's a good place to hide, he'll know where it's at."

"He might."

"This better stay between us. No Johnny Boy."

"Don't worry," she said. "He's off on the other end of the county for a property dispute. Man built a fence. Neighbor says it's on his land. Thing is, they're fighting over two inches. Fence runs a quarter mile. Neighbor says that adds up to eight hundred yards of land he's getting stole."

"Both of them ort to get a new survey," he said.

"Neither one has the money for that. All they've got is dirt and guns. That's why Johnny Boy's there and not me. He can talk to people."

"And that's why he can't know what we're doing."

Mick left the SUV, walked to her side and waited until she lowered the window.

"What now, damn it?" she said.

"Make sure and text me right after you call the FBI."

"What are you up to?"

"Complicated."

He went to the truck and drove out of town, heading for the isolated ridges that marked the Carter County line. At the foot of Tucker's hill, he downshifted to granny-gear and headed up the steep incline. A copperhead stretched itself the width of the road to capture heat. The truck provided sufficient ground vibration to alert the snake into retreat. At the top, Mick made the sharp turn that led to the dead-end ridge and Tucker's house. A white dog trotted around the house, gave a single bark, and stood before the house with its ears laid back, scruff up, and tail stiff. A minute later the door opened and Mr. Tucker emerged in work clothes, his right hand partially concealed behind his back where Mick knew he held a pistol.

"Mr. Tucker," Mick yelled from the cab. "It's Mick Hardin. I was up here a few days ago."

The old man nodded. Mick left the truck, watching the dog, who didn't appear to favor the situation.

"Didn't see your dog last time," Mick said.

"Naw, he was off on business."

"He bite?"

"If I say so, he'll tear your leg off and beat you with it."

"Can I talk to you a minute?"

"I reckon."

Tucker waved him to the porch and Mick climbed the steps, deliberately ignoring the dog.

"What's your dog's name?" he said.

"I mainly call him Dog. Makes it simpler for both of us. I've had seven dogs named Dog. My wife likes an overlap, a pup when one gets old, but it'd be confusing. Dog One, Dog Two. No end to it."

Mick nodded. The old man was more talkative than last time, and he figured it was morning coffee and a solid sleep.

"Sleep good?" Mick said.

"You ain't here to talk about sleep and dogs."

"No sir, I ain't. It's about Nonnie Johnson. I got a line on who did it. I believe he's hiding somewhere in the hills. Town's too small. You know this land better than anybody. Where you reckon he's holed up at?"

A hummingbird poked its beak in the purple blossom of a morning glory. A rival bird dived toward it and they began a mid-air duel until one flew to a chaste tree.

"There's caves," Tucker said. "Kids go in them and drink."

"Might not be private enough."

"Three or four old homeplaces nobody lives at. Roads are growed over."

"Can you show me where they are?"

"Can't leave my wife that long. I know the family names."

"That would help."

"Caudill. They's gobs of them, but Boyd Caudill's mom is the one you want. The old Branham place. And some Gibson land. All them people are gone but where they lived is still there. About like this place one day."

"My opinion," Mick said. "You got some years left above ground."

"My wife don't."

The old man cut his eyes briefly toward the door. It was rare that anyone in the hills lived into their eighties, especially a couple.

"I'm sorry to hear that," Mick said.

The old man said nothing and Mick walked to his truck. He had often imagined a life like this for Peggy and himself—finishing their days side by side on a porch, quietly enjoying the birds, trees, and flowers. He wanted to measure time by the growth of trees.

Chapter Seventeen

A natural leadfoot, Linda loved speeding over the black-top with the lightbar flashing. She enjoyed the power of the SUV, its willingness to grip the blacktop tightly, and top a hundred in a quarter-mile straight stretch. The road was officially County 519 but was locally known as the Clearfield Road, the Poppin Rock Road, or the Going-to-Paragon Road. It ran south past family cemeteries and fields of corn, following Lick Fork Creek to the community of Zag. She slowed as she approached the county line. The emergency call had designated a gravel lane this side of Morgan County with a Grand Prix in a ditch. Two people were unhurt but "not acting right."

Linda found the road easily, her car raising a billow of white dust on the crushed limestone. The Grand Prix had missed a sharp curve and gone into the ditch. The color of the right rear quarter panel didn't match the rest of the car, having been added from a junkyard. Patches of Bondo had flaked away to the raw metal in various spots, each leaking lines of rust as if weeping red tears. She ran the plates. The car was registered to Roger Crawford, a name Linda knew as a small-time seller of weed. She parked and approached the vehicle. A young man lay asleep on his side in the back seat, hands tucked between his drawn-up knees.

Two people in their early twenties sat on the ground with their backs against a downed tree. Their clothes were dirty, both shirts marred by burns from cigarettes. The woman's head lolled back against the bark. The man watched Linda as if nothing could surprise him.

"Roger," she said. "That you?"

"Yep."

"Who's your little friend here?"

"My sister."

He nudged the woman with his elbow and she looked around like a child waking from a nap.

"What's your name," Linda said.

"Shawna," she said. "I go by Shana."

"Uh-huh," Linda said. "Looks like you all ran off the road. Who was driving?"

"Me," Roger said, "but it wasn't my fault."

"What happened?" Linda said. "Deer run in front of you?"

"No," he said. "It was his turn to drive."

"Who?" Linda said.

"Jackie."

"Guy in the back seat?"

"Yep," Roger said.

"Who is he?"

"Jackie Ray," Shana said. "He's my boyfriend."

"Uh-huh," Linda said. "I see. It was your boyfriend's turn to drive and Roger wrecked. Is that right?"

They both nodded and smiled, and Linda understood they were too high for mere weed. It had to be opiates.

"You all got any drugs on you? Or weapons?"

"Yeah," Shana said.

"No," Roger said.

"Well," Linda said, "which is it."

"Pills but no guns," Roger said.

Shana nodded eagerly as if expecting a reward for a correct answer.

"Let me have them," Linda said.

In slow, jerky motions they dug into the pockets of their jeans and handed over opaque plastic containers. Linda examined them. Both were from the same pharmacy in Tampa, Florida, prescribed by the same doctor. Sixty milligrams of OxyContin, fifteen pills per bottle. Each had five missing.

"You got any more in your car?" Linda said.

"Yep," Roger said.

"Okay. I'm detaining you. Don't try to run off or I'll have to arrest you. You want that?"

They both shook their heads without speaking.

"Good," Linda said. "Stay here."

She walked to the car, knowing they were too stoned to run. The front floorboard had a coffee can full of cigarette butts. In the glove box she found four candy bars and twenty-four vials of OxyContin, the prescriptions filled at four different drugstores. She opened the rear door. On the floor was a half-eaten cheeseburger and an empty container of Oxy. With a sense of dread, she prodded Jackie, then pressed her fingers to his carotid artery and felt no pulse. She tugged his arm but rigor mortis prevented it from moving which meant he'd been dead for a few hours.

She went to her car and requested an ambulance, then called the State Police. She returned to Roger and Shana, wondering how long they'd been driving with a dead man in their car.

"Roger," she said, "I got to ask you. Y'all coming back from a run to Florida? Get some Oxy?"

"Yep."

"I had the idea you were a weed man only."

"I was," he said. "People want Oxy now."

She cuffed him, helped him to his feet, led him to her car, and went back for Shana.

"Help me understand something," Linda said. "You said it was Jackie's turn to drive when your brother ran into the ditch."

Shana nodded encouragment.

"I don't see how the wreck happened," Linda said.

"Jackie wouldn't wake up."

"Uh-huh. What'd y'all do?"

"Roger pulled on this road and slowed down but I couldn't get Jackie awake. Roger, he reached back over the seat to shake him. The car, it run off the road."

"Then what?"

"I don't remember. You got here."

"Okay," Linda said. "I'm going to have to handcuff you and you can sit with Roger in my car. Put your hands out."

Shana complied and Linda pulled her up. She weighed less than ninety pounds. Linda opened the rear door and helped Shana into the back of the SUV.

"What about Jackie?" Shana said. "He coming, too?"

Linda closed the door without answering. She searched the car again to ensure she hadn't missed anything before the State Police arrived. A tattered highway atlas. Three empty packs of cigarettes, a lighter, a packet of ketchup, four stale French fries, and a corpse.

Unwilling to wait with her prisoners, she went to the downed tree they'd leaned against and sat on it. She felt sadder than she had in a long time. Shana would sober up in jail and learn her boyfriend was dead. A court-mandated rehab program would be hard-pressed to help her recover from such a loss.

Linda adjusted her position to face the trees. It was possible to turn her back on one small part of the world at a time. The powerful drum of a beak against dead bark carried through the woods and she scanned the overstory for a pileated woodpecker. It flew a series of arcing loops and landed in the boughs of an ash tree. Below it grew crinklefoot ferns. A row of Queen Anne's lace swayed in the ditch. As a girl she'd turned them red and blue with food coloring in cups of water. The stems absorbed the water and transferred the dye to the lacey white flower-heads. She wondered if kids still did that, if Shana ever had.

Chapter Eighteen

Halfway to town Mick parked beneath a sycamore and retrieved his cell phone from the glove box. A text from his sister said:

Rest stop. FBI. Done.

Thirty minutes later he drove up the dirt road to Mrs. Kissick's house. She sat on the porch wearing an apron over a blouse and blue jeans, smoking a cigarette. One cuff was rolled up and she used it as a receptacle in which to flick her ash. Mick parked and her expression clamped down as if a lever had been thrown.

"You can go to hell in a gourd," she said.

"I probably will," he said. "Came to give you a message for your boy."

She withdrew a Colt .22 from a patch pocket on the apron. Mick hadn't seen that model in a long time. Known as a hooker's gun, it had a two-inch barrel and no hammer to snag the fabric.

"Tell your son," Mick said, "not to use the rest stop on the interstate for exchanges. The FBI is watching it."

"I don't know what you're talking about."

"Ma'am, we're past lying to each other. I'm trying to help you."

"Why would you do that?" she said.

"You helped me last night."

"That don't make us friendly."

"No, but it makes us even."

He slowly executed a three-point turn and drove up the road, watching her in the rearview mirror. She stood, tucked the gun away, and stretched her foot over the edge of the porch. Leaning on the handrail, she bent down and uncuffed her pants to empty the ashes. The soft gray haze drifted on a breeze.

Mick headed for the county courthouse. Rocksalt was a town of 7,500 that had begun in the 1800s as a transportation point serving the extraction industries of timber, clay, and natural gas. Now it had two main employers—Rocksalt State College on the east end of town and St. Claire Medical Center on the west. As each grew, the downtown area shrank, replaced by a multitude of parking lots.

The original Main Street stopped abruptly at a metal guardrail and Mick pulled over to get his bearings. A new road had been constructed on the south side. It was called Wilkinson Boulevard, named for a governor who ran a Ponzi scheme that landed him in court where he invoked the Fifth Amendment one hundred forty times. Now he had a road named for him—a bypass to a town already passed by for a century.

Mick called his sister.

"What?" she said.

"I need two topo maps. One recent, one fifty years old or so."

"The damn land doesn't change."

"The roads do," he said. "You have them or not?"

"At the office."

"I'll meet you there."

"I'm in transit right now," she said. "Courthouse, then the jail."

"Thought you let Tanner go?"

"There's a young girl I'm trying to help. Shana Crawford. Her boyfriend OD'd."

"I know the family but not her."

"Can't talk right now," she said. "I'll have Johnny Boy bring the maps outside."

"Tell him I'll be there in ten minutes."

"Anything else?"

"Yeah," he said. "What's this new bypass for?"

"Lord knows," she said. "There never was anything to do in Rocksalt, now there's more things not to do."

She ended the call. He drove to the sheriff's office and parked at the far end of the lot, nose out for a quick departure. Town lay in the widest spot between hills that rose like walls on either side. Mick was texting his sister to hurry Johnny Boy along when someone pecked on the side window. He dropped the phone and moved his hand near his pistol. A skinny young stranger stood in the lot wearing a cheap sports coat with a necktie and gun belt. He resembled a fledgling salesman at a car lot with a history of being robbed. Mick peered over the top of the open window.

"Roll it down," the man said.

"Can't," Mick said. "It's stuck. Got a pair of vise-grips in here for a handle."

"I'm Special Agent Wilson," the man said. "FBI."

"Nice to meet you."

"And you are?"

"Right now," Mick said, "I'm minding my own business."

"You're parked at the sheriff station. That makes it my business."

"Now I could be wrong," Mick said, "but I'm pretty sure the FBI investigates federal felonies. This is state property. And sitting in a truck is not a felony."

"I need your identification, sir."

"I believe you need cause for that," Mick said. "Kentucky does not have a Stop and Identify statute. Unless you think I committed a crime. Is that your idea? That I did a felony and came straight to the sheriff's office."

Wilson blinked rapidly. The tint of his face was gradually darkening. Mick could sense his frustration and wondered how things would transpire. The agent didn't seem like a man who'd drag Mick out of the car and frog-march him into custody.

"Do you have business here?" Wilson said.

"Yes, I do."

Wilson was clearly waiting for Mick to continue. Mick waited. No need to make it easy on the man who'd locked up Tanner Curtis, but messing with the agent bored him already. The front door of the office opened and Johnny Boy ambled across the lot with a bundle of maps.

"Hey, Mick," he said. "How's your mule bite?"

"Hurts a little, but not infected."

"See you met our FBI man," Johnny Boy said. "He was in the army, same as you."

"Where'd you serve?" Mick said.

"DC mostly," Wilson said. "You?"

"Oh the usual—Iraq, Afghanistan, Syria."

Johnny Boy smirked and passed the maps through the window.

"Linda said to give you these."

Mick nodded his gratitude then looked at Wilson.

"Always good to meet a fellow veteran," Mick said.

He left the lot, heading to the courthouse, which had been converted into a community center for the arts. He got directions to the new courthouse west of town. Inside, he requested property deeds and was escorted to the documents room. The records began in 1880 and he worked his way forward, seeking transactions that involved the family names furnished by Mr. Tucker.

He started with Caudill, the most common name in the county, which sent him to a twenty-year-old computer in order to access births. There were so many Caudills that it took him five hours to find Boyd then track his parents back through time to the family's first property purchase in 1939. The older topographical map allowed him to roughly locate the land and a road. The more recent map informed him that the county had never annexed the road. It functioned as a three-mile driveway and no longer appeared on maps or GPS.

Hungry, he drove through town and back, seeing only fast-food franchises. Jimbo's was long gone and the Dixie Grill, too. Pat's Poolroom had sold the best cheeseburgers but it was shut down. Metal chairs and a table stood in front of the old movie theater and he noticed a neon sign depicting a cup of coffee with a rising curl of steam. Inside he ordered soup and a sandwich, remembering Saturday matinees there as a kid. The contractor had done a good job renovating what was essentially a gigantic room with a sloped floor and no windows. Two other businesses shared the space—a yarn shop and a bookstore, the first one in the county. He purchased a jar of homemade blackberry jelly.

He returned to the courthouse and went through the same process with Branham, simpler due to the scarcity of the name. He found a Gibson property not far from Mr. Tucker's place. He'd start there tomorrow. He was stiff from sitting and poring over documents, squinting to read the handwritten deeds and birth certificates.

He fought off the impulse to get drunk in the woods and went to his own house for the third time in two weeks.

The driveway was a cracked slab of cement lined by forsythia and a black vinyl downspout extension that had been
run over at least twice. The familiar street held the same
neighbors, their cars parked in the same spots. His house
was the same, too, at least on the outside.

Chapter Nineteen

Many women experienced pregnancy as a joyful state with colors appearing brighter and smells more intense. Peggy's mouth tasted funny, she couldn't sleep well and she was exhausted all day. She felt guilty for hurting her husband. A few nights back she'd seen his truck parked across the street under the willow and had frantically tidied the house and changed clothes. She made tea and spent several minutes choosing where to sit. The couch so he'd join her? Or would he know she'd picked that spot on purpose? Mick could instantly read situations. Better to take her standard chair facing the TV with her phone at hand.

When he drove away after two hours, she'd been disappointed then angry, emotions she quickly applied to herself. She wanted to blame him for being less than generous, but could only blame herself. She loved Mick. She was the source of his suffering.

Earlier she'd worked in the garden, battling the squash bugs attacking her cucumbers. The walking onion was walking farther and farther. Her bean shoots had spread to the chicken wire fence and a few climbed the sunflower stalks. She'd greeted a corn snake relaxing on the compost heap, docile in general except against enemy rodents, qualities that reminded her of Mick. He'd have made it a pet.

They'd known each other since high school and gotten married young. Despite a higher percentage of infidelity among military couples, the subject was never talked about on Unit Family Days or in Spouse Resilience classes. The women talked about it privately in their cramped army housing. Peggy had always felt sorry for them, regardless of who cheated on whom, and thought it would never happen with her. Now she judged herself more severely due to her previous condemnation of other women. She'd become the kind of person she despised—disloyal, a betrayer, Judas.

Stop, she told herself, focus on something better. But there was no escape from her mind or the changes wrought in her body. She couldn't drink to cope with her sorrow and she couldn't turn to Mick. All her best memories were tied up with him. They'd once vacationed on the Amalfi coast of Italy where the salty Mediterranean Sea buoyed their bodies. They drank wine in the afternoons and ate late suppers of fish and pasta. The mountains rose dramatically behind the hotel. They took a bus to Ravello, a three-mile ride of dangerously twisting roads. The traffic seemed choreographed—cars barely missing each other, motorcycles passing through tiny spaces, pedestrians boldly crossing anywhere. Italian drivers were either the best in the world, or the worst. When she told Mick, he'd said people thought that wherever they lived, but in Italy it was really truly true. The phrase "really truly true" became part of their private lexicon.

Now Peggy was scared. Scared for herself, her marriage, and for the baby. She feared a bleak future—unemployed and pregnant with no man in the picture, a cliché of daytime TV talk shows. She made a supper of frozen salmon from the IGA, sweet potatoes, and yogurt. Protein was supposed to be good and she could at least control her diet. If nothing else, the baby would be healthy.

She heard the old truck in the driveway and went to the door, listening to him scuff his boots on the porch. She opened the door. He stood with a forlorn expression, clear eyes, and tense jaw. She backed into the room to avoid turning away from him and sending the wrong message. He offered a pint jar of jelly with a handmade label.

"Brought you this," he said. "One of them Ronzo family farms, I don't know which bunch is into berries."

"Odie and them," she said. "Thanks."

She carried the jar to the kitchen and tarried by the sink. She felt fragile but needed to be strong for both their sakes. She returned to the living room where he stood in the center, slowly turning, reacclimating to home—the couch, their two easy chairs, a cobbler's bench turned into a coffee table, photos on the walls from their travels in Europe. He sat in his chair and she took the couch.

"I'm glad you came," she said.

"Do you want out of the marriage?"

"No."

"Did you do it to make me leave?"

"No, nothing like that."

He nodded and she waited. Mick's directness was his best quality as well as his worst, lacking tact or diplomacy, a family trait. They'd long ago agreed that he'd never apply his interrogation skills to her. She hoped his promise still held but had no illusion that it would since she'd violated his trust.

"How are you feeling?" he said.

"Tired a lot. You?"

"Not bad," he said. "Linda's got me running around."

After a brief silence they both said the other's name simultaneously then stopped talking. She pulled a cushion beneath her arm.

"Go ahead," she said. "You first."

"I want to know everything."

"It was a guy at work. He'd been giving me the eye for months, the usual up-and-down looks and little comments. You know what I mean. I always ignored it. He was flirty. It was like middle-school bullshit. Harmless. A dumb way to pass the boring time. I liked the attention. It made me feel younger."

He nodded, focusing his vision on the wall behind Peggy in the hopes that his lack of eye contact would encourage her to continue.

"Don't work me," she said. "You can look at me."

"Okay," he said, staring at her straight on. "How'd it happen?"

"One day Lowe's closed for inventory and me and him were counting paint. Every bucket, every color. We started talking. No more flirting, just talking. He played in a band and was always broke. He was married and regretted it. His wife gained a bunch of weight and she didn't think she looked good. They hadn't had sex in a year. He kissed me and I said no. I pushed him away, Mick. I did. A few days later he kissed me again. I felt sorry for him. It just happened."

"How many times?" he said.

"Three."

"Why'd you stop?"

"It wasn't right. I knew it but didn't know how to stop. I'm sorry, Mick. It was wrong. I don't know what happened. None of it felt real. You were gone so long and I didn't like my life. It wasn't about him. It was like I wanted to be someone else. Another self with another life. It was so stupid."

She watched him roll his shoulders to relieve tension, then tip his head until his neck popped. He was trying hard and she was grateful.

"Where's he live?" he said.

"Owingsville."

"Did you bring him here?"

"No, never. It was at work after everybody left."

"At a lumberyard? Where, on a stack of plywood?"

"They sell patio furniture."

"Oh, Peggy."

His tone lost its former crispness, a slight shift that gave her a glimmer of hope. She felt suddenly hungry. In Italy people ate lunch then talked business over tiny cups of coffee, the food having softened any ire between them. She wished they'd done the same.

"Are you hungry?" she said.

"No. Did you tell him you were pregnant?"

"Yes. He quit work the same day. I never saw him again."

"What about the paternity test?"

It was the question she'd been dreading. The longer she waited before answering, the sooner he'd figure out the answer and could brace himself. Too long would be cruel.

"Not yours," she said.

He sat immobile. He didn't know if two minutes passed or twenty minutes or an hour. His eyes began to sting and he understood he needed to blink. He looked at his hands resting on his legs as if they belonged to someone else, tools set aside for future use. Twice he tried to speak but his throat felt compressed.

"I'm sorry," she said.

"I trusted you."

"You still can."

"How?"

She didn't answer. Mick understood that she'd hadn't considered this before—the significance of the effect on him. He knew her, knew that she'd focused exclusively on her own sense of guilt and sorrow, ignoring the consequences for him. It was why she hadn't told him.

"What are you going to do?" he said.

"I don't know."

"Hard to raise somebody else's kid. A man you barely know. The kind of man who'll fuck another man's wife while he's away."

"It's not genetic."

"Yeah? What do you know about him? His family? Nothing. You don't know a damn thing about half that baby in you. A musician who married up and slept down."

He watched a wave of anger tighten her face. It wasn't vengeance he wanted to inflict but something else. He wanted her to fully comprehend the situation she'd put him in. They'd groped along through twelve years of marriage, each decision the best at the time, based on available information. Now she'd discarded everything. A battlefield calm settled over him. His perceptions sharpened.

"What do you want?" she said.

"It's a little late to think about me."

"No, it's not."

"You didn't eight months ago."

"Yes, I did," she said.

"Can you stop contradicting whatever I say?"

"I'm not."

"It ain't the time to pick at me, Peggy. We're not talk-ing about where to put the couch or what kind of mesh for the screen door."

"We have a storm door."

"The porch has a screen door, damn it."

Her expression reflected satisfaction that he'd gotten angry. He knew it meant she was so mad at herself that she wanted him to be, too. But it wasn't anger that he felt, it was dismay and disappointment.

"What are you going to do?" he said.

"You want me to choose, Mick? Is that it? Give the baby away and keep you? Either you or the baby? Is that what you want?"

Her onslaught of yes/no questions passed through him, easily ignored. It was a technique of control, asking a ques-tion while presenting two options for response. Lawyers and journalists did it every day. So did unskilled interrogators. In a way, she was talking to herself.

"What should I do?" she said.

"It's your body. Your life."

"It's your life, too."

"Not exactly," he said. "Not any more."

"What does that mean? Are you leaving me?"

"What I mean," he said slowly, "is that I don't know what you've been thinking about all this time. What your plan is."

"My family thinks it's your baby. Mom comes over every couple of days. She's staying away because you're home. I can't tell her the truth. Nobody knows but you."

He looked at her as if surveilling through binoculars. Her body was turned away, arms folded over her chest, legs crossed.

"At first," she said, "I decided to have the baby and give it away before you got back. I'd tell everybody it was stillborn. Then I was scared you'd get in early. I couldn't talk on the phone because I was afraid I'd tell you and I didn't want you to fly back with all this on your mind. Then Linda called you."

She shifted position, aiming her body toward him and stretching one arm across a throw pillow. He recognized her movements as relief for having told him everything. Mick believed her. He nodded again.

"And now," he said. "What's your thinking now?"

"Go to Lexington and give the baby up. I can stay with Aunt Fran. She won't tell a soul."

He nodded and stood.

"I have to go," he said.

He went outside and she heard the old six-cylinder engine turn over twice then start with a roar. The house was suddenly hers again—bigger somehow. Mick's psychic presence filled any enclosed space but never the woods or the desert or a beach. In those places he seemed to vanish and go unnoticed by people and animals. She'd never understood it.

Peggy felt better than she had in months. She'd feared his reaction and now it was over. He'd been calmer than she anticipated. She'd forgotten his nature, the pragmatic dispassion he brought to problems big or small. This was the worst and it was over. The relief lifted a burden she only recognized when it was gone.

Keeping things from Mick did more damage to her than him, created distance within herself that found expression between them. She'd always relied on him to bring her back. Talking had alleviated the anxiety and given her fresh energy.

She scooted to the end table beside the couch and called Aunt Fran. As the phone rang she began mentally compiling a list of household tasks. She'd let things slip. Seeing the house through his eyes put everything on display —a layer of dust, potato chip crumbs on the carpet, empty bowls from days ago. She'd open the windows and air out the house.

Chapter Twenty

Mick felt like a shell, as if he was outside of his body watching someone else occupy his life. He wasn't driving the truck, the other person was, the other Mick. He was angry and exhausted and lost. The thing he'd feared was true, the thing he'd avoided thinking about. The baby was someone else's.

A fragment of his mind wished he'd never come home while another part wished he'd never left Kentucky in the first place. He wondered where his home was now, what home meant. It wasn't the house he'd bought with his wife, the cabin in the woods, or the bases he'd inhabited overseas. He lived out of a duffel bag containing two sets of clothes, socks, and underwear. He couldn't recall the last time he'd lived anywhere long enough to stock the bathroom cabinet with shaving cream and a toothbrush. On his last leave to Rocksalt he'd hung a nylon Dopp kit on a towel hook. Maybe if he'd bothered to unload it and settle in, Peggy wouldn't have felt so restless when he left.

At the eastern edge of town he stopped at a construction site. The workers were gone for the day. Building material sat on pallets. Beside it was a dumpster the size of a railroad car that leaked from rusty holes in the bottom. He got out of the truck and walked around it twice. He felt like part of his mind had come unmoored and he was in danger of drifting away from himself.

He dropped the tailgate and slammed it shut, then did it three more times, meaningless action that felt substantive but not enough. Under the bench seat he found a heavy crescent wrench rusted tight at the knurl. He lowered the gate again and beat on the Ford engine block in the bed, striking it over and over until his arm hurt and shoulder ached. The jaw of the wrench broke from impact and flew across the dirt lot. He climbed into the back of the truck, crouched behind the engine, and pushed. His legs quivered with effort. He felt the strain in his arms and his back. The engine scooted along the metal with a terrible sound, gouging furrows in the bed and the gate. With a final effort, he pushed it off the truck, the momentum carrying him with it. He landed on top of the engine, his body draped over it like cloth. He wanted to cry but didn't know how. It was like a switch hidden inside him, out of reach.

He lay on the engine block for several minutes, catching his breath. He slowly stood, grateful that no one was around. His clothes were greasy from the engine, his fingers stiff from the blows with the wrench. He drove east on old 60, then began making the turns onto smaller roads, each branch narrower than the last until he left a

county-maintained gravel lane for a dirt road. He checked
the topo map. The old Gibson place lay ahead. He drove
until the road disappeared in a washout from a creek. He
parked and retrieved his gun and a knapsack containing a
canteen, compass, knife, rope, and first aid kit.

As he walked, the holler tightened until he was moving beneath boughs of hickory and maple that wove to a
canopy overhead. A squirrel watched him without fear as
if it had never seen a man before. Mick waved hello. The
road faded into heavy woods. He skirted a blackberry patch
higher than his head, and came to a wide opening at the
head of the holler. An ideal location for a house, the land
was sheltered from weather with a natural spring flowing
off the rock cliff. He saw movement and froze. It moved
again, something pale blue and he knew it wasn't an animal.
He crabwalked sideways into the woods, stood, and began
circling, staying just inside the tree line. He held the pistol
at his side.

The house had burnt down years ago, leaving a rock
chimney amid a rectangle of weeds. A man in a workshirt
poked at the ground with a stick, then stood and looked
directly toward Mick as if able to see through the foliage.
Mick frowned, knowing he was too well-concealed for
sight. The man moved into a shaft of sunlight and Mick recognized the janitor. Mick tucked his gun away and walked
across the land, brushing aside horseweed that marked an
old drain ditch.

"Hidy, Mr. Tucker."

Tucker nodded once and stepped back into the shade. He held an oak walking stick and a burlap sack. Mick stared at the ground as he walked the perimeter. There was no evidence of a cookfire or matted area for sleeping. Bent grass and a snapped off weed marked the eastern boundary.

"You come in that way?" Mick said.

"Yep. Broke that snakeroot weed you're worrying on."

"I didn't see your vehicle."

"Ain't but a half-mile walk on the ridge."

"You hunting for the killer, Mr. Tucker?"

"Naw. I'm keeping track of nine sang plants over here. Still yet need another year."

"Down by those oaks yonder?"

"Ain't saying."

The surrounding hills were steep enough to skin your nose on climbing, strung by pine and yellowwood clinging to the limestone cliffs. The only sound was a distant cicada and an occasional blue jay irritated by the presence of humans. A squirrel chittered from the first fork of the nearest oak. Mick pointed to it.

"I was just thinking," he said, "about a squirrel that acted like he ain't seen a man before."

"Could be. They live about ten or twelve years. I knew a squirrel that made it to twenty."

Mick pondered a couple of responses, then decided to let it go. No sense debating the life span of wild animals or what Tucker meant by having known a squirrel. How do you get to know one? You can hardly know a human, even your own wife.

"Who were these people?" Mick said. "The Gibsons."

"Jerry and Gayle Gibson. They was old when I was a pup. Had fourteen kids." He pointed to the ground. "Two bedrooms right there, one for the boys and one for the girls. The Mister and Missus slept in the back."

"What happened to them?"

"Typhus got half the kids. The rest left. One road out and they everyone took it. Not a one come back."

"Pretty place with a rough history."

"Not a hill here you can't say that about."

"I reckon," Mick said. "You needing you a lift home?"

"Thank ye, no," Tucker said. "Quicker on foot."

Tucker lifted his chin in a brief motion of farewell and vanished into the woods as if the trees welcomed one of their own. Mick walked to his truck thinking about sixteen people living in four rooms, the parents watching their children die one by one.

He drove out of the holler and crossed the county on a series of back roads. After consulting the map, he followed Lick Fork Creek to a dirt road and stopped at the support struts of a swinging footbridge that had collapsed into the creek below. There was no sign of recent traffic. He left his truck and descended the slope, using saplings to prevent falling. As a boy he'd developed a method of skidding down a hill in a slight crouch, one foot extended to steer his body through the undergrowth. His weight was on the back foot

turned sideways to act as a brake. Selection of hillside was
crucial—too sheer a slope and he'd pitch forward in a terrible tumble, too slight and gravity wouldn't pull him. He'd
gotten the idea from seeing a TV show about surfing. It had
been his favorite activity as a child.

He waded Lick Fork and climbed the opposite bank to
the Branhams' land. They were a storied bunch—three sisters
who lived together—Gloria, Loretta, and Candy. Buxom and
single, they were courted by men from three counties. People
said the perilous footbridge was how the women culled serious suitors from the sporting ones. Any man willing to cross
had good intentions. Once you were in with the sisters, you
could have a wild time, and bringing a jar of liquor never
hurt. The Branham sisters were gone by the time Mick heard
about them. Candy ran off with a man from Elliott County
who didn't mind her pointed ears. Loretta had a stroke and
Gloria took care of her until they both died.

At the top of the creek bank he circled the house. It
was surprisingly big and he figured the builder had felled the
trees and milled the lumber on the site. Wind and weather
had stripped the old tarpaper roof to shreds. Someone had
set a washtub over the chimney but the bottom had rusted
through and the metal loop sat like a giant wedding ring
around the mortared rock. A copperhead sunned itself at the
edge of the shade as if too weary to go any farther. Mick
nodded to the snake, which flicked its tongue toward the
human scent.

He continued his recon around the house and peered through each broken window. Satisfied that the structure was empty, he entered the back door. Long tunnels of hardened dirt built by mud-daubers clung to the walls. The rooms held a few broken scraps of furniture, four squirrel nests, several shed snake skins, and the scattered bones of mice and field rats. Everything of the slightest value was gone. There were no doors or wiring, furniture or dishware. The window handles were missing. A thick layer of undisturbed dust coated every surface. No one had been here in many years, certainly not a killer on the run.

Mick returned to his truck and headed toward town. The next place to investigate was close but the geography was impenetrable. He needed to make a long drive that looped Rocksalt, Triplett Creek, and Clack Mountain. He stopped for gas. While the tank was filling he pulled his cell phone from the glove box. His sister had called twice and sent a text for him to get in touch. He pressed the return button and his call went to voice mail.

He called twice more as he drove back to Rocksalt. Both times he got no service due to the terrain. As he neared town he saw a car parked in a trampled field beside the road. A man was walking a loose circle, looking at the sky, his hand to his ear. Mick pulled over and called his sister. It rang twice, then lost service. He walked in the field while pressing redial. The other man ended his call and approached Mick.

"If you stand facing that big walnut," the man said, "then turn a little to your right and take a few steps, you'll get a call through."

"Thanks."

"These damn things. First they get you hooked on them. Then they jack the prices higher than a cat's back and change the cords so you got to buy a new one. Then the damn things don't work."

"About like a leash is what it is."

"We used to have a party line," the man said. "Every house up the holler on the same telephone line. Nobody told nobody nothing because everybody else was listening in."

Mick followed the man's advice and got through to Linda. The connection was weak, her voice garbled and full of static. He was able to discern a street name and the anxiety in her tone.

Chapter Twenty-One

Mick drove to town and followed Second Street north to Knapp Avenue, surprised at how far the street had extended over the years. Newer brick homes were snugged tight against the hillside. Strands of dry dirt deposited by flooding encroached the blacktop. He passed thick piles of dislodged brush, tree stumps, and rocks. A large flatbed truck carrying logs trundled down the street, its load swaying, and Mick swerved onto someone's yard for safety. Several ruts in the ruined grass indicated that other drivers had done the same.

At a fork he saw the flashing lights of first responders to the left, and headed that way, parking well back. Two police cars, including his sister's black SUV, were parked in the yard beside an ambulance. A city cop was directing traffic while another one guarded the entry to a small house made of yellow brick. Mick asked for Sheriff Hardin.

"Busy," the city cop said.

"Johnny Boy Tolliver, then."

"Not here yet."

A plain late-model car arrived and Marquis Sledge the undertaker disembarked and walked slowly toward the house, posture erect with his head slightly bowed in deference to his work as county medical examiner.

"Hey, Marquis," Mick said.

"Mick," he answered in his professionally solemn tone.

"You know him?" the cop said to Marquis.

"Linda's brother," Marquis said. "He's all right. Unofficial deputy."

Mick followed Marquis into a living room with a couch and two chairs flanking a worn rug. Tanner Curtis lay on his back with three gunshot wounds to his torso. Blood had soaked through his clothes and seeped across the floor, settling into the cracks between floorboards. His open eyes stared without life at the ceiling. Mick recalled the nervous young man he'd interviewed in jail, then quickly shoved aside the image of Tanner Curtis alive. His status had shifted to an object on the floor.

Marquis examined the body while Mick moved about the room, mentally cataloguing its contents. A knick-knack shelf on brackets held four ceramic ducks. A bookcase with a bible, four high school yearbooks, nine romance novels, and a guide to raising chickens. On the walls were an array of family photos depicting Tanner as a baby, school pictures from first to twelfth grade, and several group pictures taken at weddings and holiday gatherings. All the relatives resembled each other except him. A photo of teenage cousins dressed in finery included Tanner, but he stood separate as if the six other kids had pulled away. Or maybe he had.

Voices drifted up the hall—his sister's urgent tone and a man with a high quivering voice. Pulsing beneath the indistinct conversation was the rise and fall of a woman weeping. Marquis offically pronounced Tanner Curtis dead, nodded to Mick, and departed. Mick squatted beside the body. Three small wounds, probably from a pistol. One hole in Curtis's shirt had a thick pattern of gunshot residue indicating the weapon had been fired at close quarters. Slightly lower on his chest was a second bullet hole with a fainter circle of speckled residue. The third entrance hole was unmarred save for slender threads on his shirt that were tinged red from blood.

A door banged down the hall and Mick saw his sister escort Tanner's parents out the back door, their expressions stoic. They leaned against each other like workhorses in harness trying to make it easier for the other. Mick moved to a window and watched Linda hand them over to a city cop. She came back in the house through the front.

"This their place?" he said. "Tanner's folks?"

"Yeah, they found him. What a mess."

"Get anything out of them?"

"No," she said. "Tanner's been staying here since we released him. They were at the grocery. I don't think they're involved in it."

"I don't either," Mick said. "I believe he answered the door and was shot immediately. First one at close range. He

back-stepped or started falling. The next two shots were a
little bit farther away."

He pointed to a small hole in the wall, fresh enough
that Sheetrock dust lay on the floor below.

"Another shot missed. Dig around in there and you'll
find a bullet."

"Wouldn't it go through the wallboard?"

"Maybe, but it's close to the edge. My guess is it's
lodged in the framing. Small caliber. I haven't turned him
over but all this blood is from exit wounds in his back. The
rounds didn't bounce around inside him. The killer used a
gun laying around the house or one he kept in his vehicle."

"Anything else?" she said.

"Marquis came and left. You'll know more after he's
finished with the body. Somebody on this street saw the
killer's vehicle."

"I asked the city cops to go door-to-door."

"Good."

"I sent Johnny Boy to search Tanner's house again."
She looked at the body, a forlorn expression on her face. "If
I kept him locked up, he'd still be alive."

"He shouldn't have been arrested in the first place.
That's on the FBI, not you."

Two young EMTs entered with a collapsible stretcher
on wheels, and bent to their grisly task. Mick and Linda went
outside. The sudden sunshine illuminating the pretty street
seemed unjust, an affront to the circumstances. Another

log truck leaking twigs and bark rolled by. It slowed for the cluster of police cars, veering onto a neighbor's yard.

"They logging back up in there?" Mick said.

"Yeah. Whole damn street's mad about it. Flash floods. A dog killed. Property damage. Two kids almost run over. The mayor says the logging's legal. He can't stop people from harvesting on their own land."

"They clear-cut these hillsides and call it harvesting?"

"Lumber trees are a crop," she said. She gestured to the grease on his clothes. "How'd you get so dirty?"

"I was hugging an old engine block."

Linda's cell phone buzzed in her pocket. She answered and listened for less than a minute.

"Bring him in," she said. "I'll meet you there in ten."

She ended the call and cussed while rolling her shoulders to ease tension that had no desire to leave.

"Somebody just confessed to killing Tanner," she said. "Johnny Boy's taking him to the office."

"Not the jail?"

"No, I need to hear the story first. I don't want to lock the wrong guy up again."

"Want me to go with you?"

"Yeah, but no more secret conversations."

He nodded, watching a pair of starlings swirl around a chimney across the street. The house had a low decorative fence and he wondered how many people had tripped over it at night.

"I talked to Peggy," he said.

"About time."

"Do you know her full situation?"

She shook her head.

"It's pretty tricky," he said.

"Way the two of you been acting, I figured that."

"It's . . ."

He faltered, reluctant to say the words aloud. He didn't know why. It made no sense.

"It's not my kid," he said.

"I was afraid of that," she said. "What the hell's wrong with her?"

"She's in bad shape over it."

"What about you?"

"I don't like it much."

She looked at him with an expression of sympathy, one he couldn't recall seeing her give him as an adult.

"I'm sorry, Mick."

"Yeah," he said. "Let's go see who Johnny Boy's got."

He walked to his truck and drove as slowly as possible, forcing himself to admire the hills, the flowers in the yards, the ornamental trees planted near the houses. One had a trellis covered with morning glory vine. It was a pretty street. Eventually it would get over the murder but not the clear-cutting on the hillsides.

Chapter Twenty-Two

Johnny Boy was unsure of procedure, in particular the decision to handcuff the suspect. He had known Bobby and his brother Billy all his life. They lived across the creek from him. Ten months separated the two brothers and they were always together. People called them "Bobby and Billy," even when referring to just one boy.

Johnny Boy didn't cuff him but sat across the room and studied Bobby who was slumped in a chair and crying. He was the same height and build as Johnny Boy and dressed the same except for the shirt. Even their hair was the same color and length. Johnny Boy had a strange sensation that with a few significant shifts, Bobby could be the cop holding him in custody.

Johnny Boy gave him a bottle of Dr Pepper, the last one in the tiny refrigerator, and hoped Bobby appreciated the generosity. It sat on the table beside a roll of toilet paper, which Bobby used to blow his nose and occasionally wipe his face. Johnny Boy made a mental note to request a supply of tissue be kept on hand in the future. Like many men of the hills he had a handkerchief in his pants pocket, a red cotton one that came in a three-pack at the drugstore. It was stiff with his own sweat and he didn't feel right giving it to another man.

"Do you want me to call anyone?" Johnny Boy said. "Your brother?"

Bobby shook his head.

"You sure about what you told me?"

Bobby nodded.

"When the sheriff gets here you'll have to tell her, too."

That knowledge released a fresh stream of tears that ran down Bobby's face as if a gasket had cracked in his head. Johnny Boy looked away. He'd seen men cry twice and hadn't liked it because it made him want to cry, too. Tears had the same effect on him as yawning. To distract himself, he began going over the potential paperwork in his mind—name, address, social security number, occupation. What was Bobby's job these days?

"Hey, Bobby," he said. "You still at Henry's Garage?"

Bobby lifted his head, revealing damp cheeks with a rivulet preparing to either drip from his face or travel backward beneath his chin. Johnny Boy wondered how tears could defy gravity. Maybe it was the salt.

"You got a brake problem?" Bobby said. "I still do a little at the house. You can bring it around."

"You're the best brake man in the county."

"Henry didn't think so."

"He fire you?"

"Naw," Bobby said. "I asked for a raise. Thirty cents an hour was all the more I wanted. He cut my hours and I quit. Can't work for a man like that."

"I don't reckon."

The front door opened and Johnny Boy stood quickly. Linda and her brother entered. She glanced at Bobby's tear-stained, swollen face, and glared at her deputy.

"You hit him?" she said.

"I did not harm the prisoner."

"Let's you and me talk private a minute."

Johnny Boy followed her into her office, leaving Mick with the prisoner or suspect or whatever he was. The crier. The brake man killer. Linda shut her door and spoke quietly.

"Which one is he?" she said.

"Bobby."

"You sure?"

"Yeah, Billy's the big one."

"Right," she said, nodding. "Tell me what happened."

"I proceeded to Tanner's house like you ordered. The door was unlocked. I entered the domicile and encountered an intruder."

"Just talk normal."

With a beleaguered sigh, Johnny Boy continued.

"I found Bobby going through stuff. I asked what he was doing. He told me he killed Tanner. Then he started in crying and ain't stopped. I called you and brought him in."

"He say anything?"

"He offered to fix my brakes."

They returned to the outer office, where Mick was leading Bobby to the men's room, telling him to wash his face. When the narrow door shut, Mick stood close enough to hear the water spraying from the faucet.

"What do you got?" he said to his sister.

"Bobby Renfro," Linda said. "He confessed."

"Want me to talk with him?"

"He's all yours."

A couple of minutes passed and Bobby emerged. They settled in the office, Mick near Bobby with no furniture between them. Linda and Johnny Boy sat against the wall with an audio recording device.

"You hungry?" Mick said.

"No," Bobby said. "Are you?"

"Not right now, thanks. You know why you're here?"

"I killed Tanner."

"Okay. Let's go back a little bit. Did you know him?"

"I knew who he was. Everybody does. I worked on his dad's car."

"You get in an argument with him? Something like that?"

"No. I heard he was staying with his folks. Then I seen them at the IGA by themselves and knew he was alone."

"Then what?" Mick said.

"I went to their house."

"Did you take a gun?"

"Yeah."

"What kind?"

"A little Colt twenty-two. Not good for much."

Mick let those words float in the air like a leaf drifting to the earth.

"So you went to his folks' house," Mick said. "Anybody go with you?"

"No, just me."

"Anybody know you was going?"

"No. I went straight there from the grocery. He answered the door and I shot him four times, then took off."

"Where'd you go next?"

"To his house."

"How come?"

Bobby closed his eyes, the slight effort of his eyelids releasing tears.

"Take a deep breath," Mick said. "I know you're upset. But the sooner we get done talking, the sooner you can go back to crying. Okay, Bobby? Will you try?"

Bobby nodded and filled his lungs with a dramatic inhale. He lifted his eyebrows to Mick as if seeking confirmation for a job well done.

"Good," Mick said. "Let it out slow, then do it twice more."

Bobby obeyed and wiped his face with the back of his hand.

"You went to Tanner's place," Mick said. "Was there a reason?"

"Yeah. I was hunting pictures of him and Nonnie."

"Why's that?"

"I was gonna tear them up."

"Did you know Nonnie?"

Bobby nodded, his lip quavering. Mick leaned closer to him and softened his voice.

"Tell me how you knew her."

"High school," Bobby said. "She was nice to me. We, you know, went up in the woods one day. And, you know . . . We did it."

"You see her again after that?"

"Yes, twice more."

"Three times total?" Mick said.

"Yeah, I thought it meant something. It did to me. Then she got married to that Johnson boy who played guitar and drove a Trans-Am."

"I guess things between you and her were done."

"Yeah, for good. My brother tried to fix me up with a McGee girl. There was a bunch of them, all of them nice, but I never done it. I couldn't be with nobody else. Just Nonnie."

"You cared about her."

"I loved her, man. I loved her. And the Dopted Boy killed her. So I killed him back. I'd do it again. I'd kill him a hundred times."

"All right, Bobby. I understand. You're doing good. One more thing, where's the gun you shot him with?"

"In my car."

Mick glanced at his sister who elbowed Johnny Boy and gave him a dirty look. He left the room with an expression of chagrin.

"Bobby," Mick said. "The sheriff is going to take you to jail now. She has to."

"Yeah, I know."

"All right. If you want to cry some more, go ahead. It won't do you no good in the pokey."

"Naw," Bobby said. "Reckon I'm done."

"Come on, now. You got to go over there."

Mick helped him to his feet and Linda guided him out the front door. Mick decided to wait for Johnny Boy. The gun would corroborate the confession and if Johnny Boy couldn't find it, Mick knew he'd have to. He looked around the room, thinking that his sister spent most of her time in here. The room lacked anything personal, nothing but a desk and chair, filing cabinets, and a photo of the governor printed on canvas with a pebbly texture. In a corner the state flag hung from an oak pole. The flag depicted two men shaking hands, one in a dark suit, representing the state capital. The other figure was dressed in the fringed buckskins of a frontiersman. Kentucky's official motto surrounded the men: "United We Stand, Divided We Fall." Mick had always considered the image absurd. No politician ever shook hands with an Appalachian except to consummate the theft of land and mineral rights.

Johnny Boy plodded into the room carrying a small revolver in a plastic evidence bag.

"Laying on the seat," he said.

"Get that boy's hands and clothes tested for residue," Mick said. "Then dig a bullet out of the door frame at his folks' house. See if it matches to the gun."

"You're not my boss."

"I can ask Linda to tell you to do it. But if you get started on it now, she'll be impressed by your initiative."

"I ain't trying to impress her."

"Not searching for the gun gives an impression. A bad one. I'm trying to help. If you don't want it, no skin off my ass."

Mick headed for the door.

"Want me to tell her where you're going?" Johnny Boy said.

"Out to the old Caudill homeplace."

"They's gobs of Caudills. Town, ridge, and holler."

"Way east. I ain't for sure where it's at. The deed is registered under Augustus. He died and his wife inherited the property. Three kids, Boyd, Virgil, and Sara."

"Boyd Caudill," Johnny Boy said, frowning. "Hang on a minute."

Johnny Boy set the evidence bag on Linda's desk and went to one of the filing cabinets. He removed a tattered manila folder, the cardboard swollen from years of humidity.

"Yep," he said. "Here we go. Caudill, Boyd. Found dead twenty-six years ago, never solved."

He passed the folder to Mick who thumbed through the typed pages. Initial crime report. Interviews. Follow-ups. Boyd had a record—two misdemeanor alcohol charges. The medical examiner's document concluded death by gunshot. It was signed by Marquis Sledge Jr., the current ME's father.

"Not much here," Mick said.

"It's what's not there that matters."

Johnny Boy pulled another file and offered it. It was sparse but similar—Rodale, William. No prior arrests. An unsolved murder by gun eight months after the Caudill death.

"You think the same guy killed them both?" Mick said.

"I was a kid when it happened. But no, I don't think it was the same killer. Word was, Rodale killed Boyd Caudill. Then Boyd's little brother Virgil killed Rodale."

"Any evidence?"

"Nope. Just a lot of talk. But right after Rodale's murder, Virgil disappeared. Nobody ever saw him again."

"Somebody kill him, too?"

"The body never turned up. Troy Johnson was the sheriff then. No direct relation to Nonnie. His notes are in there. Virgil's vehicle was gone. Two days before, he withdrew a bunch of money at the bank. Troy thought Virgil planned it all out. Killed Rodale and left the county."

"He never came back?"

"When his mother died, Troy waited at the funeral to lock Virgil up but he didn't show."

"The sister live there now?"

"Naw, after her mom died, she moved to Ohio. Her husband got a mill job up there."

"So nobody's living out at their old place."

"Not for twenty-some years. Good house and a pretty place up on a ridge. Still yet standing. I can tell you how to find it. In high school it's where we went to drink beer."

Mick listened to Johnny Boy's directions, committing them to memory, surprised at the specificity. Mick thanked him and turned away, stopping at the door.

"Hey, Johnny Boy," he said. "How'd you know about all this?"

"Some days they ain't a lot to do. I read all the old files."

"And remember them?"

"Wouldn't you?"

"Yes, I would." Mick nodded. "Good work."

Mick left and Johnny Boy listened to the old truck engine roar to life from Mick pumping the accelerator to squirt fuel to the engine. New cars didn't require it. Like everything about Mick, it was old-fashioned. Johnny Boy wondered what happened when an old-fashioned man aged. Would time ever catch up with him?

Johnny Boy read the files again. He was kin to the Rodales, a fact he'd deliberately kept to himself. If Virgil Caudill ever returned to Eldridge County, it'd be on Johnny Boy to set things square.

Chapter Twenty-Three

Mick was turning onto the street from the parking lot when he saw his sister's vehicle coming the opposite way. He pulled a full U-turn, parked beside her, and got out.

"Johnny Boy found the gun," he said. "What do you do for forensics?"

"State Police. But they're backed up for weeks. You believe Bobby?"

"There might be more to it, but he's not lying."

"Thirty years," she said. "That's a long time to pine for somebody enough to kill for."

"About the same time it takes for a tree to grow and get cut down."

"So you're a logging expert now."

"No, I understand humans."

"Other ones, maybe. But not yourself. You ort to try that."

"That's right," he said. "I need to find myself. I should do yoga and get my core grounded. What's got you eat up?"

"Them city cops. They grew up with Bobby. One of them said Tanner probably killed himself."

"Maybe he did. Maybe Bobby came in and shot him twice more to make sure."

"They're on the phone right now to Murvil Knox. He won't like it. He already chewed my ass last night for letting the Dopted Boy out. Called me at home."

"You did your job, Sis."

"Sometimes I don't like my job."

"Most people don't."

"You, too?" she said.

"Try going into a barracks and arresting a twenty-year-old man stout as a bull. That's what I did instead of being home with my wife. So no, I don't like my job. I'm just good at it."

A carload of teenagers drove by, their music roaring from the windows. They pulled into a fast-food lot and poured from the car like cattle released from a pen, three boys and three girls. Four had brightly dyed hair. The other two, male and female, wore their hair in short mohawks greased to a woodpecker's crest. In the way of small-town rebels everywhere, they conformed to each other. Mick wondered who owned the car, who paid for the gasoline and hair dye.

"Those kids," he said. "They're free as jaybirds. You ever drive around like that?"

"Sure. We called it 'cutting the gut.' Drive to one end of town, turn around and go back. Our record was ninety-three. We were trying to hit a hundred but the driver had to go home and eat supper. You ever do it?"

"I lived too far out to have any buddies. Sometimes I think that's why I joined the service, to get some friends."

A late-model Ford Explorer with heavily tinted windows entered the parking lot. It rolled to a stop and Special Agent Wilson slowly disembarked. He stretched his back like an old man getting out of bed, then twisted his neck until it popped on both sides. His skin had gone pasty. Mick recognized the signs of a prolonged stakeout in a vehicle. They all three looked at each other, waiting for someone to talk.

"Sheriff," Wilson said. "I hear you got more trouble."

"And I hear you're assigned to surveillance on the interstate. You make an arrest?"

"No. My boss shut down the rest stop. Saves the taxpayer two ways—maintaining the building and paying me to do nothing."

"Tough on blind people," Mick said.

"What?" Wilson said.

"The money from those vending machines at rest stops. It goes to the blind."

Wilson looked at Mick as if he were a pup who'd shit on the porch, then switched his focus to Linda.

"Now I can assist your investigation," he said.

"Don't need it," she said.

"My orders are to offer federal help."

"Last person you brought in is dead."

"You shouldn't have let him out."

Linda sprang toward him as if launched from a cata-pult, her face red, both fists rising to attack. Mick stepped between them. He wrapped his arms around Linda and walked her backward across the blacktop lot.

"Get the fuck off me," she yelled. "Quit it, Mick."

He released her and lifted his arms, hands open.

"Ain't worth it," he said.

"It is to me."

"Beat on me all you want, but don't hit a Fed."

She struggled to regain composure, her hands shaking with rage. She began a pattern of slow breathing that he recognized from her teen years. She called it the 5-3-6: a five-second inhale, hold for three seconds, let the air out for six. A school counselor had taught her the technique after Linda engaged in a schoolyard fight. Her opponent, a boy bigger than her, had called their father a drunk and she'd beaten the holy hell out of him because it was true. Later the boy tried to date her.

The color of her face receded to its normal ruddiness, the result of too much weather and her refusal to wear makeup or sunscreen. She spoke through teeth clenched tight together.

"Get him out of here."

Mick nodded, watching her walk to the office. He considered warning Johnny Boy with a quick text but his phone was tucked away in the glove box. He turned to Wilson who stood in the stance of a boxer.

"Don't worry," Mick said. "You're safe with me."

"Attempted assault on a federal officer. I can have her in court."

"You bring charges and I'll say you initiated it."

"You'd do that? You'd lie under oath?"

"For her, yeah."

The ire leaked out of Wilson, slow at first, then in a rush like a board bowing under heavy weight before it broke. Mick almost felt sorry for him. Wilson didn't like his job, either.

"Look," Mick said. "You collared the wrong guy and now he's dead. It's the sheriff that looks bad, not the FBI."

"Who killed the Johnson woman?"

"I'm working on it."

"Let me help," Wilson said.

"Not a good idea."

Mick walked to his truck and left.

Wilson felt trapped like a mouse with no choice but to nibble the cheese. He envied Mick's loyalty to his sister. Wilson's only sibling was a brother six years older who'd bullied him unmercifully, graduated from West Point in the top ten percent of his class, and died in Afghanistan while leading a patrol. He was buried in Arlington with a twenty-one-gun salute. Their mother received a folded flag and three posthumous medals. She retreated into depression while her husband lost himself in eighteen-hour work days. Wilson had wanted to study history and become a professor. Instead he entered the ROTC program at the

University of Louisville and received his commission as second lieutenant.

In order to spare the family any possibility of further loss, the army posted Wilson stateside. Murvil Knox, a family friend, claimed credit and demanded compensation through the arrest of Tanner Curtis. Wilson had complied. He had always complied—with his brother, his parents, and Knox. He hated himself for his innate passivity.

A sense of despair settled over him like a quilt made of concrete. If his brother had come home, things would be different. Wilson would have his PhD and be working to secure tenure. Instead, the reward for his academic prowess was getting sent to a small town he didn't like, ordered to help people who didn't like him.

Chapter Twenty-Four

Peggy's mother was an overly tidy woman, one of many traits that irritated her daughter. During her visit earlier they'd eaten a muffin and drunk tea in the small kitchen, and Peggy's mother left not a single crumb or a drop spilled. She'd patted her lips with a napkin then refolded it. Peggy was glad to see her go. Her mother had never approved of Mick due to his family: parents divorced, mom a shut-in, father a drunk, grandfather a hermit. In her mother's view, Mick had dragged Peggy out of the county to places she didn't belong. The only thing her mother gave Mick any credit for was the pregnancy. Finally, she'd said. Thank God, she'd said.

Peggy wiped the table and rinsed the dishes. She repositioned the chairs as if trying to conceal all evidence of her mother's visit. She feared her mother's judgement, which would eventually arrive, an onslaught of silence sprinkled with comments of petty cruelty. Peggy wished her father was alive. He'd died on her sixteenth birthday, the worst blow of her life. Peggy married Mick three years later.

Now, at the juncture of what she suspected was the end of their marriage, that seemed significant. She wasn't sure how. She'd been young and eager for the adventure of travel, which quickly wearied her. Mick was a good man, as steady as her father, able to endure difficulty without complaint. He worked hard and came home cheerful. Even now, when she'd provided him sufficient reason for fury, he kept his temper in check. Another man would scream that she was a whore and slam his fists into the walls. Another man would show his emotions if for no other reason than a display of caring. She knew he loved her, that his steadfast loyalty would never wilt.

Peggy had never been the kind of woman who rushed toward a baby, eager to hold one, cooing over its tiny hands. Friends with young kids were perpetually fatigued, often complaining, their houses messy. Nevertheless, she wasn't convinced of giving the baby up for adoption. It was growing inside her own body, a preposterous thought in the abstract, but the concrete reality was something altogether different. More than anything it was hers, hers alone. She'd felt its movement for the past three months, increasing in frequency at night. She'd told no one about that. She didn't want to share the thrilling sensation with her doctor, her mother, or Mick. It was her baby.

Peggy sat on the couch and played a game on her phone, dozing against the cushion. She preferred being asleep, the only time she had a break from the discomfort of her body and her rushing thoughts. The door knocked twice and opened. Linda came in.

"Oh," Linda said. "Sorry to wake you."

"No," Peggy said, "it's okay. I was just resting a little."

Linda placed a takeout bag from a Mexican restaurant on the table.

"You still craving tacos?"

"I don't know. Maybe. Thank you. I just had a snack with Mom."

"How's she doing?"

"Getting on my nerves mainly."

"What do you tell her about Mick staying at the cabin?"

"Not much," Peggy said. "She'd rather visit when he's gone anyhow."

Linda settled in her usual chair. She and Peggy had been close in the past, closer than now anyway, and she tried to stop by every couple of weeks. She hadn't since Mick's return. Learning that he wasn't the father had changed everything Linda had thought before. She understood Peggy keeping it secret, but now that Linda knew, she felt awkward, as if she was concealing information.

"How's Mick?" Peggy said.

Linda considered how to answer, then realized that they always talked about Mick. Not Linda's work or Peggy's mother or local gossip. Just Mick. Linda wondered if she and Peggy had anything else in common.

"He told me about the baby not being his," Linda said.

"Yeah, well. It's true."

"I didn't think it's something you'd lie about."

"What's that supposed to mean?"

"Nothing," Linda said. "I'm glad you told him."

"Are you mad I didn't tell you?"

"No," Linda said. "I'm mad that you hurt my brother. That's what I'm mad about. How could you do that?"

"It was an accident. A mistake."

"That's what teenage girls say. You're thirty-three years old. You know better. He's tore all to pieces about it."

"You shouldn't have told him."

"He needed to know."

"My decision, Linda. Not yours. You stuck your nose in and now you're in my house criticizing me. I didn't want him to see me like this. I had a plan and you ruined it."

"What plan?"

"Have the baby and give it up before he got here. It'd be easier on him that way. Easier on both of us. But no, you had to go and call him. Him being tore up is your fault."

"You're his wife. You're supposed to talk to him."

"What do you know about it?" Peggy said. "You've never been married. Longest you ever had a boyfriend is what, six weeks?"

"Eight months."

"Oh, right. That Collins boy from up Brushy. I remember him. You broke up with him because you didn't like the way he ate."

"He scraped his teeth on his fork."

"It's always something with you," Peggy said. "That Jackson guy, let's see, he bit his fingernails. And Orville Carter, you said he dressed too nicely. Who am I forgetting? Bobo Fraley drove a car you didn't like. Leonard from the sawmill, he liked to watch too much TV. One of them Anderson boys, I forget which one, you didn't like his haircut. Did I say anything? No, never. Not my business if you want to get a reputation."

"A reputation for what?"

"You tell me, Linda. You're the one who dated half the guys in the county."

"At least I used a condom."

"All that means is you planned it out ahead of time. You're no better than me so don't act like it. When you've been married fifteen years to a man who's gone most of the time, I might pay attention to what you have to say. Till then, stay out of my life."

They stared at each other, both angry, both afraid of what the other might say. Neither knew how to head things off.

Linda stood and moved to the door.

"You were like a sister to me," she said. "What happened?"

"I got bored," Peggy said.

"Of me?"

"All of it. This house, Rocksalt, Mick being gone. Every day I do the same things and have the same conversations with the same people. They're always watching and judging. Never to your face but you can feel it. Now you and everybody else has a good reason for it. When was the last time we talked about something personal?"

"We are now."

"Too late," Peggy said. "Everything's too late."

"Mick came back for you."

"He won't stay."

Linda left, already thinking of the responses she could have made. Things she should have said. Mainly she felt bad for having lost a friend. She didn't have many and she'd known Peggy for twenty years. Peggy was too young for a midlife crisis but they came early in the hills. Everything did—death, hardship, and loss. Usually kids, too. Maybe after the baby was born she'd settle down but the impact of ugly words would stick around. Peggy's assessment had stung because it was true. Linda constantly evaluated men, seeking reasons to rule them out. No one was ever good enough.

All the complaints Peggy had about life in Rocksalt were the same reasons Linda liked it. The security of seeing the same people, sometimes three times in a single day at different stores. There was a protocol for such encounters. The first time you asked about family. The second time you smiled and made a joke about running on the same schedule. The third time you smiled and waved. It created an intimacy that felt safe. Part of the reason she liked law enforcement was a desire to maintain order for everyone, an order that Peggy no longer cared about.

After Linda left, Peggy sat on the couch and cradled her belly. She was angry with Linda and mad at herself, mad at everyone except the baby. She was surprised by what she'd said, thoughts never articulated or acknowledged. She'd been supremely bored and had been for a while. Well, she wouldn't be after the baby was born. Being a mother would give her purpose, one that didn't wane like being a wife or a sister-in-law. Linda had a career and Peggy would have a baby. It's what she wanted.

Chapter Twenty-Five

Mick drove east on country roads, glad to get away from the whole mess of civilized life. He missed the simplicity of the army. Time had a malleable quality in the desert, as if it ran slow or not at all, then jumped ahead or receded two centuries. Life there was similar to the hills. He'd missed the color green, shade thrown by trees, and even humidity. Now he yearned for the desert's crystalline air and the solace of vast empty space.

He stopped to consult his map, hand-drawn following the plat he'd photocopied at the courthouse. Johnny Boy's directions had helped—up old 60, right at Open Fork past the creek, left on Bearskin, keep going over Crosscut Ridge then look for a gap in the trees. It led to the old Caudill place. Mick continued east, thinking about the Caudill brothers, Virgil and Boyd. He wondered if every family history was that sad, or just in the hills. Appalachian people lived by old codes that compelled them to take action. Affronts were always personal. Acts of vengeance maintained themselves through generations. Before school started each morning

Mick had recited the Pledge of Allegiance and the Lord's Prayer. Every child learned the words: "As we forgive those who trespass against us," a strong and generous message that neglected to include a timeframe. In the hills it was handier to forgive trespassers after killing them.

Bearskin was a single-lane blacktop road that had been dirt when Mick was a kid. At the end of the holler, he ascended the steep winding slope to Crosscut Ridge. The top of the hill caught a breeze that cooled his face as he watched for the space between the trees wide enough for an old road. He stopped twice. One turned out to be a gap left by past loggers and the other was a natural break in the tree line. He continued more slowly, enjoying the beauty of the hills. The opening, when he finally saw it, was obvious and man-made. He drove beneath the canopy and parked beside a stand of evergreen that would conceal his truck from the road. He squeezed out, the pine needles scratching his face, then reached into the cab for his knapsack and gun.

He looked around carefully, memorizing the area in case he returned by a different route. This was the last place Mr. Tucker had mentioned and Mick hoped he'd find Delmer Collins here. His plan was simple—take him into custody and let Linda use him to get Murvil Knox off her back.

He squatted to examine the weeds and shrubbery mashed by a recent vehicle. Each blade of grass was still bent in a slight arch, meaning the tracks were from earlier in the day. The distance between the tires indicated a large pickup truck. A few feet farther he saw another set of slightly older tracks beneath the fresh ones. Mick entered the woods and moved parallel to the old road, stopping every few steps to listen. A bobwhite announced its name as if introducing itself to the woods. An early owl called. In two hours full night would arrive, the darkness heavy and thick, the canopy of interlocking tree limbs blocking starlight. His impulse was to rush so he slowed his pace.

At the top of a slight rise he stopped in mid-step, keeping his arms and face still. A truck stood in the remnants of the road, a late-model Ford F-150 four-by-four, the same one he'd seen parked at the Johnson house. Whoever had parked there wanted to approach the old Caudill homeplace on foot.

He moved slowly until seeing a section of the house through the foliage. He went downslope to a dry rain gully and crawled up the hill on his belly. The house sat in what had once been a glade shaded by massive old-growth oaks. High weeds filled the yard among clumps of fescue wide as an axe handle. The porch floor appeared solid but the roof had caved in years back. Mick backtracked into the woods and began a long slow reconnaissance of the house, circling it, moving in close to see the rear, then repeating the process with the two exterior side walls.

He sensed someone behind him and spun suddenly, pistol in front of him. Nobody was there and he heard no sound. He shrugged it off as the result of hyper-vigilance. When it happened a second time he studied the woods for three minutes, unable to shake the sensation that another human was nearby. The woods were still. A cardinal emitted its call—two quick whistles followed by chirruping that dwindled to silence. Mick knew he was alone. Cardinals only made that sound when they felt safe.

On the far side of the house was another vehicle, an old Bronco that had been refurbished. He moved closer to the building and heard the voices of two men. He couldn't make out the words so he listened carefully to the tones. One was talking faster than the other. Both were under pressure, distraught, the muted voices tinged with despair. He assumed one or both were armed.

Mick ducked behind a walnut tree and considered options. If he crept close enough to hear them, he risked alerting them to his presence. A diversion would draw them out but if they left the house together the odds were fifty-fifty that Delmer could get away. It was better to trap them inside.

Hunched low and moving slow, Mick made his way to the Bronco. He used it to shield his progress as he circled to the rear of the vehicle, which was parked beside the porch. One board was missing from the porch floor. The front door was open. He went back through his recon, configuring the house in his mind—rectangular with a second story that spanned the back half of the house. The door would lead to the front room on one side and a kitchen on the other. He needed to take two quiet steps across the earth, leap to the porch, dodge the hole in the floor, and charge

through the door. He'd be inside within four seconds. He
ran the procedure through his mind, imagining the precise
movements he'd make. Twice more he pre-visualized the
sequence of movement, then he sprang from the edge of the
Bronco and burst into the room.

Two men turned abruptly toward him, both young,
one armed with a revolver. Mick knocked the gun aside
and punched the man in the chest hard enough to take his
breath. The other man stared at him. He sat on a ladder-
back chair with a plank for a seat, his legs trembling from
fear. Mick scooped up the gun and aimed one at each man.

"What's your name?" he said to the seated man.

"Delmer Collins."

"Who's your buddy?"

"Frankie Johnson."

"Nonnie's boy?"

Delmer nodded.

"He here to kill you?" Mick said.

Delmer nodded again, glancing at Frankie who lay on
the floor gasping.

"Well, he ain't going to now," Mick said.

He prodded Frankie with his boot.

"Get up," he said. "You ain't hurt that bad. Just scared
because you can't get your breath. If I'd known it was you,
Frankie, I'd have gone easy."

Frankie scooted across the floor to the wall and leaned
against it, holding his chest. He squinted at Mick as if trying to place him.

"I been to your house," Mick said. "Talked to your aunt and cousins. You were laying in the bed at the time. Figured it would be Wade or one of the twins up here, not you."

Frankie shook his head and spoke in a voice both raspy and high-pitched.

"Wade said it had to be me."

"Why's that?"

"He killed my mom." Emboldened by an ally, he pointed his finger at Delmer. "You killed Mommy."

Delmer twisted his head to the side as if trying to dodge the truth of the words. Metal handcuffs fastened one wrist to the chair.

"You bring those cuffs?" Mick said to Frankie.

"Yeah, Wade had them."

"Get the key."

Frankie dug in his pants pocket awkwardly and pulled out a shiny silver key. The single bit at the end of the shank indicated a low-quality restraint, the kind you buy online.

"Throw it on the floor," Mick said.

Frankie complied. The key bounced twice and lay gleaming in the dust.

"You don't have to kill him," Mick said.

"Eye for an eye, tooth for a tooth. Right there in the Good Book."

"There's things not in the Bible, you know. Things that weren't around back then."

"Like computers and cars?"

"Like state prisons," Mick said. "You think about Delmer's life inside. Every man in there has a mother. They'll know what Delmer did and they won't like it. They'll bash his teeth out. They'll take his clothes and his food. All you can do is take his life. That what you want?"

"Yeah."

"Then you'll go to prison and the same thing will happen to you."

Frankie was silent, trying to sort through the information and the sudden shift in circumstance. It was too much, too fast. He wanted to go home and play video games in bed. He was afraid of Wade but this stranger scared him more.

Mick looked at Delmer and spoke.

"How long's this boy been here?"

"About an hour," Delmer said.

"An hour," Mick said. "Frankie, I don't believe you want to shoot him or you'd have already done it. That right?"

Frankie nodded miserably.

"You're a good man, not a killer. So tell me why you came for real."

"Wade said I could have the truck if I did it."

Mick grimaced. In Kabul he'd interrogated a young Afghan after a failed attempt at a suicide bomb in a market. The kid had been the pawn of older men, an unwilling dupe manipulated into sacrifice. Mick was disgusted then and disgusted now.

"Get up," he said.

Sweat ran off the ridge of Frankie's eyebrows and he wiped it away, leaving smears of dirt across his forehead. His clothing hung loose on his underweight frame. He needed a haircut and he smelled bad.

"Go home," Mick said.

"What do I tell Wade and them?"

"Ever what you want. But don't talk to nobody else, hear? Just your family."

Frankie nodded and turned away, eyes averted like a dog that had been caught messing with garbage. From the doorway, Mick watched him walk across the dregs of yard, his gait slow at first then quickening the farther he went. He crested the slight hill and descended, his body vanishing in increments until only his head was visible, then gone.

Delmer was in worse shape than Frankie—bug bit, circles under his eyes from lack of sleep, clothes filthy. A makeshift table held empty tins of tuna fish, cans of pop, and potato chips. Mick offered his canteen. At Delmer's quick nod, Mick unscrewed the cap and held it to his lips. He drank greedily until the water ran down his chin leaving streaks in the dirt.

"You got one arm cuffed to the chair," Mick said. "You could have stood up and swung that chair at him."

"I was waiting on the chance."

"You kill Nonnie?" Mick said.

Delmer nodded.

"Talk, damn it."

"It was an accident."

"Bullshit," Mick said.

"I didn't mean to. It was her idea. Something she got off the internet."

"Tell me."

"If you can't breathe it's supposed to be like cocaine during sex. That's what she said. I didn't want to do it."

"Did you?" Mick said.

"Yeah. She was older than me. Said she'd tried most everything and wanted something new. So I choked her from behind. Like those UFC guys on TV."

"While you were having sex?"

Delmer nodded.

"Then what happened?"

"She passed out and I set her down. She wouldn't wake up. She wasn't breathing. I got scared, really scared, you know?" He glanced at Mick as if seeking sympathy. "Then I ran."

"What about her?"

"I rolled her over the hill."

"You run on foot?"

"No, I drove off Choctaw."

"See anybody?"

Delmer nodded.

"Who?" Mick said. "Who'd you see?"

"Fuckin' Barney."

Mick could guess the rest but he wanted it confirmed.

"Did you go home?" he said.

"No."

"Where'd you go?"

"Uncle Murvil's house. He told me to hide up here. Said he'd fix things."

Delmer's face brightened with a sudden thought. Briefly he felt relieved. He was safe.

"Hey," he said. "Did my uncle send you up here?"

A board creaked outside and Mick sidestepped, pivoted on one leg, and dropped to a squat, gun aimed at the doorway.

"Hidy," said a man from outside. "Hello the house."

The boards creaked again and Mr. Tucker stood in the doorway, silhouetted against the afternoon sun. A burlap bag was slung over his shoulder. He held a ginseng root in one hand, the long tendril still dark with soil.

Mick lowered his gun and stood. Tucker entered the house, instinctively scraping the soles of his boots on the mat that wasn't there.

"Mr. Tucker," Mick said. "You've not showed up at the best time."

Tucker tucked the ginseng in his bag. He pulled out a snub-nose .38 and shot Delmer three times in the chest. Delmer pitched backward, pulling the chair with him. He flailed on the floor with red foam frothing from his mouth. Blood spread across the floorboards. Mick knew he was bleeding internally. He squatted beside Delmer and applied pressure to the entry wounds, a futile act but worth a try. He watched the boy die, then stood and faced the old man.

"You've put me in a bad spot," Mick said.

"Naw, I believe that boy laying there did. I saved you some work."

"Why'd you shoot him?"

"Nonnie was my wife's second cousin."

The flat finality of Mr. Tucker's tone was hard as iron. Mick recognized it from his own grandfather, the same hill-bred conviction of vengeful purpose. If Mick had stayed here, he'd be the same way. He'd gotten out and missed it terribly but every time he returned he wanted to leave again. He could drive away and be done with the whole thing or he could take Tucker into custody.

"How's your wife?" Mick said.

"Doctor give her a week."

"You want to be with her when she goes?"

"Reckon I do."

"Then get on home," Mick said. "Keep your mouth shut about me being here."

Tucker nodded and turned away.

"Wait a minute," Mick said. "Was that you out in the woods when I come up on the house?"

"Yeah."

"I didn't see you."

"You weren't supposed to."

"How'd you do that?"

"I don't know," Tucker said. "Just always could."

He dropped his chin in farewell then left the cabin and entered the woods. Mick watched him go, wondering what kind of man Tucker was before he started janitoring at the grade school. One thing for certain, he was no stranger to killing. He'd shot Delmer as easily as swatting a fly.

Mick pulled his shirt from his pants and used his knife to cut off a section of its tail. The key still lay on the floor. Holding the handcuffs with the fabric of his shirt, he unlocked Delmer from the chair. He wrapped the cuffs in cloth and slipped them in his knapsack along with Frankie's gun and the key. Four sets of boot prints marked the dusty dirt of the floor. The house lacked a broom. Mick removed his shirt and swept his tracks, walking backward to the door. A discerning eye would realize someone had cleaned the crime scene but he figured whoever found the body would make their own mess. At the door he noticed the diminutive print of Mr. Tucker's foot. He wiped it away.

Mick stood in the yard looking at the house, the weathered siding, broken windows, and patched roof. He thought about the Caudill family—one brother dead, the other long gone, and now a corpse inside. If any house ought to be haunted, it was this one.

Chapter Twenty-Six

Mick drove out of the woods and parked on the blacktop, then spent several minutes obliterating his tire tracks. An hour later he arrived at the Johnson property, honked the horn, and waited. The sun had slipped behind the western hill, cloaking the house in shadow. The big F-150 was parked in the yard. A mockingbird began calling. The ultimate misfit, it could only copy others and hope for understanding. Mick had felt that way all his life.

A curtain inside the house moved as someone peered out. A few seconds later Wade stepped onto the porch. Mick left the truck.

"Hidy, Wade," he said.

"You ain't welcome here."

"No, I don't reckon. Thing is, you need to talk to me."

"I got nothing to say."

"I do," Mick said.

"Say your piece and get off our property."

"What I got to say is to everybody. You, the twins, and your mom. Frankie, too. Don't worry, it ain't bad."

Wade stared at the maple where the mockingbird continued its effort to find a friend. He spat in the yard, then shrugged to himself.

"I hate that damn bird," he said. "Comes here of the evening every day. Aggravating as hell but Mommy won't let me kill it."

They entered the house and Mick nodded to Lee Ann, who sat in a rocking chair with a floral cushion. Wade gathered his brothers. The twins gently helped Frankie to the couch, solicitous as nurses. Mick looked at each of them. Their faces had a serious intensity. Mick spoke.

"You gave Frankie a gun and put him on Delmer. I sent Frankie back home. We're all in this and I aim to get us out. But we got to work together."

"What about Delmer?" Wade said.

"Delmer's dead."

The family's collective tension eased a little, producing a slight calm like the aftermath of hard weather. Mick watched them conclude that he'd killed Delmer. He was counting on that. They'd be afraid of him.

"Frankie was never there," Mick said, looking at Wade. "He can't ever tell anyone he went up there."

The family looked at each other, nodding.

"Frankie," Mick said. "You understand what I'm saying. You weren't there. That means you didn't see me up there. You never saw Delmer. If you tell anybody different, they'll lock you up for a long time."

Frankie nodded and Mick turned to Lee Ann.

"Ma'am," he said, "you might have to remind him. All of you will. If he says anything, it'll be bad for everybody."

"All right," Wade said.

Noel and Joel muttered their assent.

"You hear the man, Frankie?" Lee Ann said.

Frankie nodded without lifting his eyes.

"Thank you," Lee Ann said to Mick.

"Don't thank me yet," Mick said. "I ain't done. They'll find the body one day and come around here. I'll keep Frankie out of it but you got to keep me out, too."

"Anything else?" Wade said.

"No, that's it."

Mick nodded to each man in turn, then faced Lee Ann.

"Frankie ain't able to kill anybody," Mick said. "I believe he's a good man. With time, he'll pull out of this. Take care of him."

Mick left the house with Wade following. The night was silent, the mockingbird having carried its loneliness elsewhere. Mick opened the truck door and picked up his knapsack. From it he withdrew the scrap of cloth that held the handcuffs.

"These cuffs have got Frankie's fingerprints on them. Yours, too. I've got the pistol you gave Frankie. You bring my name in and my sister gets the cuffs and gun."

"You'd do that?"

"I'd do a whole lot worse. Especially to a man who tried to trade a truck for a killing. You understand what I'm saying?"

Wade nodded and Mick got in his truck. He drove out of the holler with the windows open, listening to crickets and cicadas. At the blacktop he removed his cell phone from the glove box to call Linda. He'd tell her a partial story, one that didn't include Mr. Tucker.

His phone had a voice mail from his wife and three texts from his sister. Peggy was at the hospital.

Chapter Twenty-Seven

Mick sat with his sister in the waiting room of the St. Claire Medical Center. Linda explained that Peggy's water had broken early and there was concern about the baby's health. Due to the complication Mick was not allowed in the room with his wife.

"They might have to take the baby," Linda said.

"Take it where?" Mick said. "Lexington?"

"No, it's what people say. It means a Caesarean birth. They do it to protect the baby. Supposed to be safer."

Mick's sole experience with professional medicine was the dismal conditions of VA hospitals and base clinics. This one was cleaner. The waiting area had comfortable chairs, vending machines, and a TV with no sound. Other people sat anxiously nearby. A palpable tension hung in the room despite the cheerful decor. Each time a nurse passed, everyone stared in the hopes of receiving information.

"You know this hospital is named for Dr. Louise," Linda said. "They say she delivered ten thousand babies before they built this place. Claire's her middle name."

Mick nodded.

"She wasn't a saint," Linda said. "There's a real Saint Clare with a different spelling. That Clare's the patron saint of television."

"TV has a saint?"

"Yeah, she watched mass on it when she was sick."

"How do you know something like that?"

"I used to date a doctor here. He was from Philadelphia. Talked real fast. Thick accent and hard to understand sometimes."

"I guess it didn't work out with you and him," he said.

"Larry wasn't here long. He was part of a program for doctors with big med school bills. They go somewhere that needs doctors, here or Indian reservations, the Mississippi Delta. They work a couple of years and the loan is forgiven. He finished and took a job in Wisconsin. Wanted me to go with him."

"Why didn't you?"

"I told him I had to stay and help Mom but that was a lie. The truth is I don't want to leave."

"Sometimes I wish I hadn't. This whole thing is my fault—Peggy in here, I mean."

"Don't blame yourself."

He nodded.

"Larry had a lot of funny stories," she said. "One he told me, a man brought his wife into the ER. She'd been bit by a snake. Larry asked what kind of snake. He said it was the funniest thing—"

Her phone buzzed. She answered it, talking quietly, and left the room. Mick knew she was trying to get his mind off Peggy and was grateful, even if it was impossible. His own nervousness surprised him. Jumpy expectant fathers were normal but the kid wasn't his. Maybe it was the environment. He disliked being indoors, and hospitals were the worst—few windows, bland colors, busy personnel walking swiftly with quiet steps.

Linda returned, her face distraught, the skin tight, her mouth a sharp line like a surgical slit. He looked at her and waited.

"That was Johnny Boy," she said. "I need to talk to you. Not in here."

He followed her along the wide corridor through a maze of intersecting wards with nurse stations at central points, each leading to another hall. They took the elevator down and walked through the new pavilion and finally outside. Two orderlies were smoking cigarettes and looking at their phones. Linda continued into the parking lot until she could speak privately.

"Bobby's dead," she said. "Hanged himself in jail."

Mick nodded.

"I should've seen it coming," she said. "Warned the jailer."

"Now you're blaming yourself," he said.

"Maybe it's what we do. Why we both wound up in these kind of jobs."

Mick walked to the middle of the parking lot. He looked east, then west, and finally at the black hillside that shadowed the town. The moon was a crescent of bone.

"There used to be a road here," he said.

"You sound like Papaw."

"This hospital takes over everything around it."

"The college does the same on the other end of town. Pretty soon there won't be nothing else. Progress is wrecking us."

"Now you sound like Papaw," he said.

The raucous noise of an eighteen-wheel truck gearing down echoed from the interstate connector. Behind it came the high-pitched whine of a motorcycle. Tendrils of cloud slid across the sky like smoke. Mars was in its place as if lodged in a socket. Nonnie's death had produced three more—Tanner, Delmer, and now Bobby. The vulnerable always died early. Death begat death, and he'd been unable to halt its advance.

He went to the edge of the parking lot where a line of sweetgums and wild roses twined around the strands of a wire fence. Beyond it was a small house built of wood. The hospital or college would take it soon. Mick felt like the house, trapped between powerful forces. His career and his personal life were being squeezed together with no room for him. He felt suffocated by his family, the town, his marriage, even the tiny cabin in the woods.

Linda's pocket buzzed, the light of her phone blinking through the fabric of her pants. She reached for it and Mick walked away, not wanting to hear about the next loss. Frankie, he thought, it would be him. The people who were supposed to protect him saw him as an instrument to use, and now he'd be a liability.

"Mick," his sister shouted. "It's a girl!"

They trotted across the asphalt and returned to the maternity ward. A nurse explained that labor had been short and fast. The baby was healthy, small but not classified as premature. Peggy had received epidural anesthesia, then a dose of hydrocodone. The baby was in neonatal care and would be moved to the newborn nursery soon. The nurse warned Mick that for the next few hours Peggy would be groggy and weak.

Mick entered the room and saw her propped at an angle on the bed. He stood at a distance, aware of his dirty clothing, his recent proximity to murder.

"You're here," Peggy said.

"Yeah," he whispered. "Yeah, uh, uh . . ."

She gestured to a couch beneath a window. Instead he pulled a chair next to the bed and took her hand.

"I'm glad you . . ." she said. "I didn't think . . ."

Her voice trailed away and her eyes closed.

"It's all right," he said. "I'm here."

Her breathing shifted into the steadiness of slumber, her hand still clenching his. Various medical machines emitted a lulling hum that relaxed him. He wanted to remain in this untroubled state forever. He could retire from the army and open a boat shop on Cave Run Lake. Peggy had mentioned it years ago. He'd dismissed the idea out of hand but when the desert heat reached 115 degrees he often imagined sitting on a chair facing the water. In a few years he could teach the girl to fish.

He dozed, awakening when nurses came and went. A doctor entered, examined the machines, and left. Then another nurse. Then his sister.

"Mick," she said. "Mick, wake up. We've got a problem."

Instantly alert, Mick followed Linda into the hall. A woman in scrubs pushed a food cart along the immaculate corridor. From an open door came the excited hubbub of a family seeing the newest addition to their ranks. Standing at the far end near the nurse's station were Johnny Boy and Special Agent Wilson.

"It's the FBI guy," she said. "He's here to arrest you."

Mick nodded, wondering if Delmer's body had already been discovered. Tucker wouldn't have talked. It must have been the Johnsons. They'd given him up.

"What charge?" he said.

"AWOL. The army issued a warrant. I got notification, too."

"Why didn't you tell me?"

"I was going to," she said. "Then Peggy came here and I decided to wait."

"Where's the nursery?"

She raised her hand in a halt gesture to Johnny Boy then led Mick the opposite way. They rounded a corner and entered a room with a large glass window. On the other side were rows of transparent cribs with high sides like aquariums. Four were empty. The rest held babies—most sleeping, some wired to monitors, two crying. Taped to the side of one was a placard that read HARDIN, GIRL.

Mick stared into the room for a full three minutes, memorizing the contours of the box and position of the infant. Her face was tiny and red. Hair the color of her mother's wisped from beneath a white cap.

"She's beautiful," Linda said.

"I need to tell you a few things."

"Best hurry. I don't know how long Wilson will wait."

"Delmer Collins is dead," he said.

"Who killed him?"

"There won't be any more killing. That's what matters."

"Where's the body?"

"The old Caudill place," he said.

"What else is up there?"

"Delmer's car. No evidence. No shell casings. No footprints."

"You did it, didn't you?"

"I cleaned it up. But I didn't kill him."

"Fuckin' Barney?"

"No, not him. With the rest stop shut down, he'll need a new place to meet. If you find it and put a stop to the whole thing, those bigshots will leave you alone."

"You got it all worked out, don't you?"

"Not really," Mick said. "I wish I could've brought down Murvil Knox."

"Who killed Delmer?"

"I can't tell you now," he said.

"When?"

"After the guy who killed him dies. Right now I need a favor."

"What?"

"Tell Peggy I forgive her."

"Anything else?"

He looked through the glass at the pink sign: Hardin, Girl.

"Yeah," he said. "Tell her I'm not coming back."

They left the room and walked the bland hallway. Johnny Boy appeared miserable while Wilson's eyes gleamed with purpose.

"I have to take you in," Wilson said.

"Let's see the papers," Mick said.

"They're in the car."

"I've got mine," Linda said. She pulled a sheaf of documents from her jacket pocket. "They faxed them over. It's all official, Mick."

She gave Wilson a tight smile lacking any trace of humor.

"He's my prisoner," she said.

"The FBI has jurisdiction," Wilson said.

"No, you don't," Linda said. "You're here to assist. That's what you told me. Your boss Murvil Knox made it clear to me."

"He's not my boss."

"He brought you here. You report to him. You're his pet Fed."

"My orders come from the Louisville office," Wilson said. "Right now I'm placing your brother under arrest for Absent Without Leave. It's a federal offense. I'm a federal agent."

"I'm the high sheriff of Eldridge County." She slapped the warrant against her open palm. Her voice hardened. "And you are interfering with my duties."

"You'll regret this," Wilson said.

"Just add it to the pile," she said. "The biggest regret I got is being forced to work with you."

She took a step forward, moving within arm's length of Wilson. Mick had seen this sort of standoff dozens of times, motivated by pride, ego, and arrogance. Self-righteous people were the most dangerous. Worse, they were unpredictable. Linda took another step and Wilson backed off.

"Sis," Mick said. "Maybe you should let him do it."

"Hush a minute," she said. "Let me think."

The hospital intercom requested a doctor to the ER. A nurse pushed a cart with a computer attached, the wheels rolling silently. The four of them stood in a tense circle with several people watching.

"Johnny Boy," she said, "your phone got a camera on it?"

"Sure does."

She nodded, still thinking, then looked at Wilson.

"I'll cuff Mick and lead him out," she said. "Johnny Boy will take a bunch of pictures of us, Mick and me only. When we get outside, I'll turn Mick over to Wilson. He'll get the formal credit and out of my damn hair."

"Why the photos?" Wilson said.

"Johnny Boy will show them around. Get one in the paper. Everybody will know it was me that took him in."

"Smart," Mick said. "Makes good sense politically. You'll be the sheriff who arrested her own brother."

"Might get the mayor off my ass."

"They'll all be afraid of you," Mick said. "That's good."

He looked at Wilson, waiting. He knew Wilson would pretend to think it over long enough to preserve a thin shred of dignity. Twenty seconds passed before Wilson shrugged. Linda latched the handcuffs around her brother's wrists. The four of them walked down the hall, Wilson in the lead with Johnny Boy moving backward and firing off multiple bursts of photographs. Mick deliberately kept his face turned to the lens.

After a silent elevator ride, they took the long way through the hospital, past people Mick recalled from high school—patients, nurses, orderlies, and intake clerks. The older woman selling flowers from a small alcove had known his mother. Everyone saw him in custody of his sister. Word would spread through the county. It probably already had by social media.

They walked across the parking lot to Wilson's car. Linda removed the handcuffs.

"What now?" she said to Wilson.

"Stockade at Fort Campbell," Wilson said.

He reached for the handcuff case clipped to his belt.

"It's a long drive," Mick said. "No cuffs. I give you my word I won't escape. Or we can let the sheriff get the arrest. Your choice."

Wilson nodded reluctantly.

"Sis," Mick said. "You'll look back on this as the best day of your life. You finally got me under control."

"Maybe," she said, and forced a grin. "Probably."

As a group they went to his grandfather's truck where he retrieved his knapsack. He gave the truck keys to Linda.

"Tell Peggy what I said."

"All right," she said. "Hey, Wilson. Stay the fuck out of my county."

Mick grinned and nodded to Johnny Boy. He walked around the car and waited for Wilson to unlock it. The trip took nearly six hours with a stop for food and gas. Neither man spoke.

During the drive Mick realized his marriage had ended years ago except for shared household projects. He'd thought that was enough. Perhaps he was naïve. People married when they were young and optimistic, then grew entangled like rosebushes or grew apart like weeds. He believed that he could have withstood her dalliance with another man, something physical that lacked emotional involvement, but a baby was another matter. They'd lived apart for more than half their marriage which meant they both preferred it that way. He considered it a personal flaw to flee when things got hard.

He wanted to be the kind of person who'd accept the child of another man. It was noble and honorable. But he knew that every time he looked at the kid he'd think of his wife's betrayal. Mick didn't want his resentment and sorrow to work its way into the life of a child. Given his history, he'd be a terrible father to his own kid let alone that of a stranger. His marriage was over and he was leaving the country in legal jeopardy. Worse, he'd been unable to stop further murder. He'd failed on all fronts.

Chapter Twenty-Eight

Fort Campbell straddles the state line of Kentucky and Tennessee, home to the 101st Airborne Divison and the 5th Special Forces Group. Mick had gone to jump school there and later completed the FRIES/SPIES course to learn insertion and extraction from hot zones. Wilson called ahead for clearance but they were arriving at 2300 hours which meant driving an extra twenty minutes to Sabre Gate. As soon as they entered base, Mick's body instinctively relaxed. He was home.

Wilson followed Mick's directions to the building that housed the 502nd MP Battalion. They left the vehicle and stretched. A corporal completed the paperwork for prisoner transfer and gave a copy to Wilson.

"Corporal," Mick said. "Turn your back."

"Sir?"

"I outrank you. Turn your back."

Frowning, the corporal shifted his body to face away. Mick delivered a swift right hook to Wilson's stomach.

Air blew out of his lungs and he doubled over, trying to breathe. Mick leaned close to him.

"That's for Tanner Curtis," he said.

The grinning corporal escorted Mick to the office of Lieutenant Colonel McVey, commander of the stockade. The room was plain and simple in a way Mick preferred. There was an American flag, a photograph of the president, and a large insignia of the CID crest with its motto:

Do What Has To Be Done

Mick felt more comfortable than he had in the past three weeks. Despite not being in uniform, he saluted and stood at attention.

"At ease," the colonel said.

Mick moved his left foot parallel with his shoulder, tucked his arms behind his back, and interlocked his thumbs. The colonel looked through a file, occasionally giving Mick a shrewd glance.

"Chief Warrant Officer Michael Hardin," McVey said. "Know why you're here?"

"AWOL, sir. Pregnant wife. She gave birth this afternoon."

"Congratulations. But that's not the reason."

Mick nodded once, waiting.

"Your CO wants you back pronto. A triple-homicide at Camp Darby in Italy. I'm to put you on the first available aircraft. Got a flight in two hours. You're lucky. If you got here any later you'd have to wait a week under guard.

You have time for chow and a shower. You could use some clean clothes."

He studied Mick carefully.

"What's wrong with your arm?"

"Mule bite, sir."

"See the medic."

"Yes, sir."

"That's an order, Chief. In Afghanistan we used them to transport M240s, ammo belts, and Javelins. Mean animal. Carry disease."

McVey leaned back in his chair.

"Have a seat," he said.

Mick sat in the wooden chair opposite McVey's desk.

"I was stationed at the Rock," McVey said, using the affectionate term for Garrison Baumholder in Germany. "Pretty country. Fun town. Good beer. I know your commander. Colonel Whitaker is the best man I ever served under."

"Yes, sir," Mick said. "Same for me, sir."

"Your record is impressive." He opened the file. "Soldier's Medal. Silver Star. Purple Heart. Highest clearance rate in the CID. If you get tired of Europe, I can use a man with your abilities."

"Thank you, sir."

"Dismissed."

Mick stood, saluted, and moved to the door, stopped by the colonel's voice.

"One more thing, Chief. Say hello to my men on duty."

"Sir?"

"You're a legend in CID. Some of them applied due to your example."

"Yes, sir," Mick said and left the office.

Two hours later he boarded the plane with new clothes and a fresh dressing on his arm. After takeoff he slept for three hours. The rest of the way he pondered the anecdote that Linda hadn't finished telling him, the woman with a snake bite in the emergency room. Like a puzzle, he considered it from different angles. It was probably funny, or took a funny turn, but he couldn't figure it out. There was nothing funny about a snake bite.

The End

Acknowledgments

For generous time and assistance with military details, I am grateful to Sergeant First Class Levi S. Houston. For assistance with details of law enforcement, I am grateful to Major Jim Hyde, Ret., Bowling Green Police Department. Any and all errors are mine and mine alone.

For generous support and editorial feedback, I thank the following people: Amy Hundley, Nicole Aragi, Kathi Whitley, Randy Ryan, Bill Boyle, Michael Farris Smith, Ivo Kamps, Diana Schutz, Ari Friedlander, and Levi Henriksen.

I'm also indebted to former and active members of the Haldeman Mafia in the hills of eastern Kentucky.

Most of all I thank Melissa Ginsburg—poet, novelist, friend.

Read on for an excerpt from Chris Offutt's
next Mick Hardin novel,
Shifty's Boys

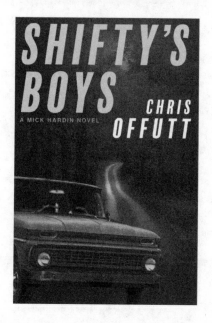

"Offutt captures the nuances of those who call this
part of eastern Kentucky home . . . [with] crisp
dialogue, bits of humor, an evocative look at the
region and a stalwart hero."
—Oline H. Cogdill, *South Florida Sun Sentinel*

Available in hardcover and ebook.

Chapter One

At age eight, Albin decided to be a race-car driver when he grew up. He assembled model cars, cobbling together pieces from various kits to make his own hot rod—number eleven, painted in green and white. He imagined himself as the youngest winner of the Brickyard 400, with enough money for ice cream every meal. It never occurred to him that at twenty-two years old he'd be driving a cab in his hometown of Rocksalt, Kentucky.

Half the job was sitting in the car waiting for dispatch to call. The rest was driving roads he'd traveled thousands of times in the past eight years—blacktop, dirt, and gravel. A county map was imprinted on the inside of his skull. All he had to do was mentally glance at it to know the best route. He had a few regular fares, severely inebriated men leaving the only two bars in town. The bulk of his customers needed a ride to a doctor's office or home from the hospital. He relied on them for income and felt momentarily

disappointed when they recovered, which he knew said
something awful about himself.

For the past six hours he'd been on duty with no calls.
He cruised the small college campus, worthless at night,
but he was bored and getting desperate. Main Street was
deserted. He drove by the new jail, another waste of time
because nobody got released after dark. The bars were just
getting active, and it'd be several hours before the drunks
started leaving. He called dispatch to double-check that his
cell phone was working and got chewed out for tying up
the line.

Rocksalt had a few places that were suitable to waiting
for a fare. A drugstore parking lot in the middle of town
was best, but twice he'd been stiffed by pillbillies who'd
spent all their money on legally prescribed opiates. It was
time to find an isolated spot, take two hits off a joint, and
enter his long-term fantasy of being a race-car driver. All
it took was a big-shot promoter passing through to hire his
cab and recognize Albin's skill at the wheel.

He'd bought his first go-cart at Western Auto, a company that went out of business several years ago. Albin had
loved entering the store from the rear and descending the
steps to the sales floor. It was the only indoor vista in the
county, one he'd marveled at as a teenager. Now the asphalt
parking lot behind the store was pocked with holes, some
deep enough to damage his car's suspension. Fast-food bags
littered the surface along with empty pop bottles. He carefully steered to his favorite place, snugged against the old

door, its glass replaced by a sheet of plywood. The roof cast a shadow that would conceal his cab. An odd shape lay in a corner of the lot, and Albin flicked on his brights. Somebody was sleeping against the dilapidated fence, somebody who could use a ride home.

Albin left the car, something no cabbie liked to do, and walked toward the man, who lay on his back. One arm was twisted beneath him, the other outstretched as if reaching toward Albin. Dark splotches marred his clothing. Albin thought it was mud until getting closer and recognizing dried blood. He stumbled to his car and called 911. Then he hid the half joint in the cell phone charging slot built into the dashboard, glad he hadn't smoked before the cops arrived.

Chapter Two

Mick Hardin awoke from a dream in which he lay in his childhood bed and couldn't move. His eyelids felt weighted, and he wondered if he was already dead and someone had placed pennies over his eyes. The coins were supposed to hold eyelids shut and serve as payment to the ferryman who transported the dead across the River Styx. Mick lay awake remembering the IED attack that had sent him to an army hospital for three weeks. He'd been released and ordered to rehabilitate his leg, a grueling and painful ordeal. From bed he'd moved to a wheelchair, then shifted to crutches for three months. He'd graduated to a cane that embarrassed him in public.

His commanding officer, Colonel Whitaker, presented him with a special cane intended for soldiers. The lightweight aluminum was painted black, with a slogan down one side: "This We'll Defend." Because the words were printed vertically, the apostrophe was a tiny pip, and the motto appeared at first glance to be "This Well Defend." Every time Mick used it, he remembered the old well at his grandfather's cabin in the woods, the water cold enough to numb his gums. He rehabbed his leg until he could limp around the base on his own, then asked to go home for the rest of his medically mandated leave. His wife would look after him and could drive him to the nearest VA hospital, eighty miles away in Lexington. The colonel agreed and ordered Mick to keep his cell phone on and return all calls. Mick nodded and flew home.

Now he opened his eyes. He was in his mother's house, not the cabin where he'd spent his formative years. He felt fatigued, his limbs heavy, a product of the pain medication. He'd gone from fentanyl on the battlefield to morphine in the hospital to Percocet upon discharge. He was still taking it, although the pain no longer required that level of management.

He'd lied to Colonel Whitaker. There was no wife to provide Mick's care. They'd separated a year ago. The divorce papers were in Mick's luggage, unsigned, along with his cell phone, switched off. He was waiting for a reason to complete the documents and sever himself from sixteen years of marriage. Despite the circumstances, it didn't feel right. Neither did sleeping at his mother's house in a spare room. Mick's sister, Linda, had inherited the house when their mother died. Linda was at work. She was county sheriff, running for election, and he didn't see her much.

The bedside clock said ten thirty, and Mick knew she'd be home for lunch soon. He had enough time to walk his daily two miles for the reward of Percocet. He left the ranch house at the deadend of Lyons Avenue and set a strong pace. In several neighboring yards were clumps of forsythia that glowed yellow, cheerful in the spring sun, their fronds already tinged green along the edges. Jonquils were blooming. On the hill overlooking the street, he could see the haze of redbud and a few pink dogwoods. The hills were gorgeous in all seasons, especially spring, when the land offered such promise and hope. Its beauty plowed him under. Mick's life had come undone to a great degree, and here he was licking his wounds under his dead mother's roof, tended to by his tough sister. The absurdity of the situation cheered him momentarily.

A neighbor woman waved from her flower bed. Two dogs trotted around another house, the entire back half of their bodies wiggling a greeting. He gave them a walking scratch, reluctant to break his stride. His leg hurt, but it felt good to put his limbs to work. He was mostly healed. Daily exercise was the final stage of rehab, intended to rebuild the muscle mass he'd lost from lying for weeks in grim hospital beds. Across the street was Miller, the mail carrier, a man Mick knew from high school. His was one of the few federal jobs in the county, and more than four hundred people had applied. Everybody wondered how Miller had gotten the position.

Mick silently cursed his bad timing—now he'd have to chat with every person on the street who was retrieving their mail. Sure enough, Old Man Boyle lingered by his box, watching Mick approach. He wore creased trousers, tan loafers, and a shirt buttoned to the collar, as if he'd dressed for the occasion of leaving the house. Bull Boyle had served in Vietnam and lost a son in Iraq. He maintained a certain sympathy for Mick, wrapped in a shroud of resentment that Mick had come home more or less intact. Above each of Boyle's ears was a large crescent-shaped hearing aid of a vague tan color. Mick recognized them as old-school VA issue.

"How's the wheel?" Boyle said, pointing to Mick's leg.

Mick slowed to an amble out of respect.

"Getting stronger every day," he said. "Any good mail?"

"Yeah, I won two thousand dollars. Got to go to the Chevy dealer to collect. They'll give me a sales pitch, then a pair of earbuds. What the hell am I going to do with them? Side of my head'll look like a hardware store with all manner of equipment hanging off it."

Mick chuckled.

"Your sister all right?" Boyle said.

"Yeah, she's running me ragged. Only reason I do my walks is to get her off my ass."

"She's a good lawman-woman," Boyle said. "I'll vote for her."

"Linda said it'll be close."

"That other feller's no good. Thinks he's shit on a stick and would be if he had a peg leg." He glanced again at Mick's leg. "Didn't mean nothing by that."

"I know it, Mr. Boyle. I got to get on before it stiffens up on me."

"Good man," he said. "Catch you on the flip-flop."

Mick increased his pace, listening for the faintly audible pop of his knee or the imaginary creak in his hip. As the crow flies, it was a quarter mile from his sister's house to the first cross street, but Lyons Avenue followed a meandering creek off the hills and the route was ultimately a full mile. Twice he crossed the street to avoid people.

Their father died young, and Linda had stayed with their mother. From age eight, Mick had lived with his grandfather and great-grandfather in the woods twelve miles east. He'd never liked town. It wasn't Rocksalt specifically but clusters of people in general. Town required a social patina he was no good at, an exoskeleton of politesse. People said one thing and meant another. They became offended if you dared to be honest and direct. It was as if saying what you thought was forbidden. He preferred the forthrightness of country people and army life.

Lyons Avenue ended at Second Street, a name that always amused Mick due to its lack of imagination. In big cities, such designations made sense because of multiple cross streets, but Rocksalt had only three: Main Street, First Street, and Second Street. Mick made his turn and walked back toward his sister's house. Two cars passed, and he waved without looking. Sweat skimmed his back and legs. He was breathing easily enough to escalate his pace to a forced march, eyes straight ahead and alert to the periphery. His sister's house came into view, and he double-timed it, counting cadence in his head, one hundred and eighty steps per minute, until he made it to the driveway.

Panting like a dog, he leaned against the exterior wall and drank from the garden hose, pleased with his progress. He was nearly strong enough to return to duty. His wife of sixteen years was living in another town with another man and their child. At best he considered it collateral damage from prolonged deployments overseas. At worst, he'd failed as a husband.

Chapter Three

Sheriff Linda Hardin drove the county vehicle home for lunch with her brother. She loved Lyons Avenue, where she'd grown up. She'd learned to ride a bicycle here, gone door-to-door selling Christmas candles to raise money for her grade school, and later sneaked out for furtive cigarettes with a neighbor girl. Linda knew all the neighbors, none of whom would have predicted that she'd be the first female sheriff in county history. A natural lead foot, she always drove slowly on her own street so everyone could see the big SUV with the official decal emblazoned on the doors and a light bar across the top.

She'd had a busy morning that amounted to nothing—an empty car parked on a dirt road off Big Brushy, unintelligible graffiti on a barn, and four wild dogs chasing a loose cow. She had a court appearance in the afternoon. Not a bad life for a single woman with a good paycheck. The only drawback was her brother, who seemed to be recovered from the IED attack in Afghanistan but was still taking pills and rarely leaving the house. His presence was a palpable force, as if he filled the entire space with his wounded psyche. She loved him but preferred living alone.

She drove into her driveway and saw him leaning against the clapboards, spraying the back of his head with the hose. Water formed a cone around his face like a veil. It was as close to a bath as he'd had for days.

"Hey, Mick," she said. "Glad to see you're cleaning up some."

He nodded, making the fan of water shiver like a shower curtain. She went into the house for a towel, noting with a grimace that they were all clean and folded, as they had been for a week. She took it outside.

"I don't want you dripping in the house," she said.

He turned off the hose and nodded his thanks.

"Been meaning to ask," she said, "how come you quit taking showers? Your leg?"

"No," he said.

"Well, it's getting on my last nerve."

"Wish you'd told me that three or four nerves ago."

She chuckled.

"Well," she said, "why not?"

"I took a shower every day in the army, sometimes twice. Part of it was dust in the desert. But the real reason was never knowing when I'd have access to plumbing again."

"Yeah, so?"

"You've always got running water. Knowing I can take a shower anytime means I don't have to."

"That doesn't make a lot of sense, Big Bro."

"No, I guess not," he said. "Not much does anymore."

"That's your pills talking. Why're you still on them anyway?"

"Because I'm stuck here living with you instead of my wife. And it's better than drinking whiskey."

"Maybe it's time to go back."

"To whiskey?"

"No, to Germany and the base. The life you like."

"Not yet," he said.

He walked away, rubbing the towel briskly over his head. Linda watched him go. She worried about him, but he was a big boy, and she was more concerned with her career. Several years ago, Linda had become a dispatcher for the sheriff's office. To her surprise, she liked being part of something bigger than herself, something that was good for the county. When a deputy resigned under a sexual harassment scandal, she was offered the position. The county politicians thought the first female deputy would help offset the negative publicity. Linda reluctantly agreed, mainly for the bump in pay. The sheriff died suddenly, and she was promoted past the senior deputy, a lazy and incompetent nitwit who worked part-time at a landfill, where he'd managed to wreck three dump trucks, no easy task. He quit the force, and Linda appointed Johnny Boy Tolliver as deputy and learned the job.

She'd never intended to run for sheriff. Her plan had been to fill the post until the election, then ask the winner for reassignment back to dispatch, but a sexist moron had thrown his hat in the ring. Keeping him out of the job was crucial to her. If he won the election, it would vindicate all the men who thought a woman shouldn't have authority.

Most important, she was good at the job. Everyone knew her family history—father a drunk, mother a shut-in, brother with personal problems and hard to get along with. In Eldridge County this public information made her trustworthy. She believed she could win the election as long as her brother didn't cause social friction. On the surface he was calm and calculating, but she knew he was capable of sudden action based on intuition. Nobody could control him. Maybe she should confiscate opiates from a dealer and make sure Mick had plenty. Drugged, he wouldn't be at risk of interfering in the election. Ideally she'd arrest him for possession and ship him back to base. Grinning to herself, she went inside.

Mick had made lunch—turkey and Swiss sandwiches with potato chips and pop. A slight tension tinged their silence. He ate as if in a mess hall, arms protecting his plate, eyes on the food. Linda searched her mind for a subject to ease things, difficult because so many crucial topics were forbidden—his wife, his wounds, the drugs, now even his damn hygiene.

"Oh," she said. "Some local news I need to tell you."

He nodded, chewing.

"A body was found two days ago."

"Just the one?"

"That's right, smart guy. Thing is, you know him."

She waited for him to display curiosity about the world beyond his concerns. Instead he looked at her, waiting.

"It was Fuckin' Barney," she said.

"He still moving heroin in?"

"Well," she said, "not as of two days ago."

His quick grin was like a sudden burst of sunlight emerging from behind a rain cloud then vanishing. She felt triumphant.

"Who do you like for it?" he said.

"Nobody. It's city cop jurisdiction. He was behind Western Auto. Shot three times."

"Thought it was closed."

"It is," she said. "This ain't about the store."

"What's it about, then?"

"Dope," she said. "What else? Now wash them dishes for me, will you? And take a damn shower. I've got court."

She stood up from the Formica table, adjusted her equipment belt, and left. Mick wondered what she was riled up about. A good soldier, he followed her orders, then took a Percocet and lay on the couch. He had one more pill left. He could save it or take it now. He took it. He'd regret it tomorrow when he wanted one, but the regrets were piled up like cordwood everywhere he looked. His medical leave ended soon. Better if he was off the meds then anyhow. Still, the days would pass even more slowly without pills.

The opiates hit him—not nearly as hard as he'd like but enough to flatten his sense of time. The light through the window was pretty to look at.